CARE & CONTROL

by Roshan K. Pitteea

ROYAL PALMS
PUBLISHING

To my Blue Light Family and all the public sector workers who protect the most vulnerable in our society.

Disclaimer

This is a work of fiction. Unless otherwise indicated, all the names, characters, businesses, places, events and incidents in this book are either the product of the author's imagination or used in a fictitious manner. Any resemblance to actual persons, living or dead, or actual events is purely coincidental.

TABLE OF CONTENTS

Chapter 1

---◄◄◊►►---

"X-ray Tango one-nine?"

Louis Mortimer snapped to attention at the sound of his callsign on the radio. He had been scanning passing traffic and pedestrians from the passenger seat of a marked Vivaro police van. It was almost one o'clock in the morning, nearly home time, and his mind had been starting to wander. He rubbed his tired brown eyes then looked across to his crewmate Luke Porter, who had been completing an intelligence report on his handheld terminal.

"Here we go," murmured Luke.

Louis reached up for his radio and held down the talk button. "One-nine."

It was a few seconds before the control-room operator's voice came across the radio. Louis recognised the Lancashire twang. Susan, he remembered her name was. "One-nine, any chance you can head to City Square? Door staff at The Plum are saying they've seen a young kid hanging around with some street drinkers."

"One-nine, that's received. Show us on it," replied Louis as Luke started up the van.

"Let's hope this keeps us out of mischief until home-time," said Luke.

Louis started up his handheld terminal, which had the appearance of a large smartphone. As well as being able to use it as a mobile phone, he was able to access any number of police systems through it. He began reviewing the incident log, a running record that had been started as soon as the door staff had rung in their concerns. He scrolled down to a rough description of the kid – white, blond hair, 5'4 wearing black trackie bottoms and a red hoody. He pressed his radio button again. "One-nine, doesn't this match the clothing description of that lad missing from foster care?"

"Bollocks," muttered Luke, weaving through the light city-centre traffic. "So much for staying out of mischief."

"One-nine, yes, yes," came the response. "Connor McAllen, age fourteen. Missing from Fir Tree Gardens, Log 192 of yesterday's date if you need to look at it."

Louis acknowledged the message then looked over ruefully at Luke. "Sorry, mate."

The tall, muscular man of thirty-three years with close-cropped dark hair sighed dramatically and carried on driving towards their destination. Louis knew his displeasure was only feigned. Luke had tutored Louis through his first ten weeks on active patrol and now, nine months on, was assessing him for his final sign-off. Luke had a jovial, salt-of-the-earth way about him that often disguised the fact that he was very astute. He had joined the police at eighteen and a half, a frontline bobby through and through.

Louis was in awe of him. He thought about their first shift together. Luke had coaxed a mentally-unwell man down from a motorway bridge, speaking reassuringly to him all the while with humanity and compassion. In the same shift, they had turned up to a domestic abuse incident where the male perpetrator refused

2

to engage with Luke's repeated attempts to reason with him. When the man tried to headbutt Luke, he suddenly found himself face down on the carpet whilst his hands were being cuffed behind his back. As soon as they had booked him into custody, they were straight back out again so Luke could get a statement from the victim and ensure she had access to help. He was dedicated and took pride in his work. So, for all his grumbling, Louis knew that Luke was mentally rolling up his sleeves to get stuck in, and was probably quite proud that his tutee had made the connection.

Louis saw City Square in the distance. The large plaza had been paved with pale grey stone, brightly lit by ornate streetlights. A substantial square pool with a grand fountain in the centre stood in the middle. The square was hemmed with a variety of bars and restaurants, mostly chains. Louis wondered whether the council had been thinking of some Italian piazza. Unfortunately, the reality was nowhere near as glamourous.

The Plum was the only pub still open at this time of the morning on the square. The chilly January air had kept all but the most determined smokers indoors. Two imposing men clad in black stood at either side of the doors. One of them saw the police van pull up at the edge of the square and motioned to the mouth of an adjacent alleyway. In the gloom, Louis could make out a number of scruffily-dressed adult men.

As they alighted from the van, Louis held down the 6 button on his radio, signalling to the control room that they had arrived on the scene. Luke had pulled on his black woollen police-issue beanie. Louis wished he had done the same but it was too late now. Even under the layers of his uniform and body armour, the cold made him shiver. A loud beep told him that his and Luke's body-cams had activated.

Louis focussed his gaze on the huddle of men near the alleyway. He couldn't see any signs of a red hoody, or anyone that might be the missing boy. His right hand reached down to the holster on his hip, touching the can of PAVA incapacitant spray to reassure himself that it was there if he needed it. Louis had never come out on a shift without all his protective equipment, but there was a first time for everything. He glanced sideways, noting the bright yellow handle sticking out of a black holster on the front of Luke's black tac-vest. Louis knew that Luke wouldn't hesitate to use his Taser if the situation called for it.

A few members of the group had caught sight of them approaching and were starting to slope off. By the time Louis and Luke had reached the alleyway, those that had broken away from the group had skulked off into a nearby underpass and out of sight.

"Evening, gents!" said Luke cordially. "How are we all?"

Louis appraised each of them, five in total. All were scruffy and grizzled, reeking strongly of cheap cider.

"Alright, officer," replied the one in a dark blue puffer jacket, his eyes glassy and unfocussed. "We weren't causing a disturbance, yeah."

"Didn't say you were, fella," Luke replied, still cheerful. "The young lad in the red hoody, where's he got to?"

Louis had learnt from Luke that sometimes the direct approach was the most effective. This was one of those times. The man thrust his chin out in the direction of the alleyway. "Summat about Wilko taking him to meet someone."

"Go and have a look," Luke said quietly to Louis.

4

Louis nodded and headed towards the alley. He felt a little uncomfortable leaving Luke by himself with five alcoholics, but he knew that Luke could more than handle himself. Louis walked into the alley, his nose wrinkling as the acrid stench of urine hit him. The alley was dark, barely lit by a couple of security lights along the wall of the buildings to either side. He walked cautiously past a row of silver-coloured industrial dumpsters on his right. The smell of rotting food and sickly-sweet stale alcohol mingled in the air.

His earpiece crackled and Luke's voice came over. He was passing names and dates of birth to the control room. Typical, thought Louis. Thorough as always, Luke was checking that none of the men were circulated for arrest.

Louis couldn't remember if the alley was a dead end or whether it led out to another street. His right hand went down to his PAVA again, just to reassure himself it was within his reach. The light had faded. Louis kept walking, cautiously now. He pondered drawing out his torch. He squinted, his eyes adjusting gradually to the gloom. The alley looked to be opening up ahead. Maybe a loading bay for the pubs?

He could hear voices. An adult male one was rambling about something. She was supposed to be here, he was saying. The other voice was louder, angry.

Louis broke into a saunter, popping the press-stud on his PAVA holster open in case he needed to draw it quickly. He rounded the corner.

"You said she was going to be here!" the young, indignant voice echoed through the dark, cobbled yard.

Louis scanned the scene quickly. He spotted a youth in a red hoody

5

squaring up to a wiry man in a black hoody and dark jeans.

"Calm down, Connor mate," the older man slurred, trying to placate the furious teenager. He swished the can of lager he was holding from left to right as he spoke. "She's unreliable, her."

"Fucking idiot!" The teenager named Connor lunged at the man, shoving him hard in the chest with both hands. Even though he was smaller, he was angry enough to muster enough force to knock the man right off his feet and back against a dumpster.

"Oi!" yelled Louis, rushing forward.

Connor took off fast, the slap of his trainers on the cobbles echoing through the yard. Louis was a lean, seasoned runner but the weight of the Kevlar stab vest and his bulky patrol boots were enough to give Connor the advantage. As he ran, Connor's hood dropped from his head and Louis glimpsed curly blond hair on top and shaved sides.

A loud metallic rattle rang out along with a loud expletive. Connor had run at full speed into a chain-link fence. Louis sped up, watching Connor trying to scale it. He managed to jump high enough to pull himself halfway up, but the gaps were too small for the tips of his trainers to gain any purchase.

At nearly six feet tall, Louis easily took hold of Connor's left shoulder and right forearm, pulling him down from the fence. The stream of abuse from the thrashing teenager quickly became a series of furious roars.

"Pack it in, mate," Louis said calmly, keeping firm hold of Connor. The kid was thin underneath his hoody but literally shaking with rage. "Come on, calm down."

The shaking subsided and eventually the angry snarls gave way to sobbing breaths.

"Are you ok?" asking Louis. The kid was wheezing hard. Louis patted his pockets quickly, satisfying himself that there was nothing sharp in them. There was something else, though. "Inhaler?"

Connor gasped as Louis let go of his forearm, allowing him to reach into his pocket and pull out a blue inhaler. While Connor puffed on it, Louis looked round the yard again. The man Connor had been with was nowhere to be seen.

"Come on," said Louis, taking hold of Connor's right upper arm. "We'll go back to the van and take you home, alright?"

Connor didn't say anything. He was still wheezing a little but it seemed like all the fight had been knocked out of him. As Louis led him through the alleyway, he asked, "What's been going on here?"

No answer.

The mouth of the alleyway came into view and Louis was grateful to see Luke's imposing silhouette filling it. When they got closer, Luke greeted Connor affably. "Now then, young man."

The three of them walked to the police van, the two officers nodding to the doormen as they passed. Luke relayed to the control room that they had located Connor and would be returning him home. When they reached the van, Luke got into the driver's seat whilst Louis sat with Connor in the back. The van was equipped with a holding area, referred to as a cage, right at the back. Since Connor was not under arrest and was, in any event, calm now, Louis was happy to let him ride in the normal seats. If that had been the wrong decision, he knew Luke would have said something.

As the van set off, Louis turned to Connor and said, "Alright, let's have a chat about what you've been up to whilst you've been missing."

Connor snorted loudly and turned away.

Louis looked forward and could see Luke's eyes in the rearview mirror, shining with amusement.

"Who was that bloke that you were with?"

Nothing.

Louis waited a moment then tried another tack. "You were waiting for someone, right? Who was she?"

Connor's head turned slightly before whipping it back away.

"Your girlfriend?"

"Fuck off!" Connor snapped without turning.

Louis wasn't put off by the outburst. "Do you want to call her and tell her you're being taken home?"

"I wasn't meeting anyone, dickhead."

"Alright." Louis tried to think of the other questions in the return interview form, which was completed each time someone went missing. He could have brought it up on his handheld terminal but he didn't want to give Connor another excuse not to engage with him. In fact, Connor's non-verbal communication was more telling than what he was actually saying. "Have you come to any harm whilst you've been missing?"

"Fuck off." Deadpan now.

"Any criminal activity whilst you've been missing?"

"Fuck off."

"Where have you been whilst you've been missing?"

"Fuck off."

"Any drugs or alcohol?"

"Fuck. Off."

Louis couldn't help laughing out loud. The kid's attitude reminded him of himself giving the police similar responses when he'd been brought home as a teenager. The unexpected burst of humour caused Connor to turn and look at Louis. For the first time, Louis noticed the lad's startling blue eyes. "Alright, mate. Clearly this isn't a convenient time for you. When would suit you better?"

"Tomorrow at one," sneered Connor, making eye-contact now. "It'll get me out of maths."

"Which school?"

"Jenkatraz."

Louis knew the nickname given to Jenkinson Street Pupil Referral Unit by students and staff alike. Jenkinson Street was an alternative education provision for children who weren't able to manage in mainstream school, usually for behavioural reasons.

"Fair enough. Best get straight to bed when we get you home. It'll be time to get up and go to school before you know it."

"Red Bull, mate," Connor said with feigned exasperation.

Luke called out from the driver's seat, "Do we need to call your foster-mum to let her know we're bringing you?"

"Foster-carer, knobhead!" Connor snapped angrily. He sank back into his seat, pulled up his hood and folded his arms tightly. When he next spoke, it was with a weary sadness. "Do what you want."

Louis could see from the sat-nav on the dashboard that they weren't far away now. He decided not to try and engage Connor any further. The poor kid looked to be trembling a little, maybe through cold or something else. Perhaps the adrenaline from earlier was now wearing off.

A moment later, Luke turned the van into a new-build housing estate. Each pale-bricked cookie-cutter house was well-presented, at least one car on each driveway. They pulled up outside Connor's address. An expensive-looking black Mercedes and a brand-new blue SUV sat in the driveway. Before opening the doors, Luke gave Connor a friendly but firm warning about running off when they let him out. Connor rolled his eyes.

Louis got out then stood by whilst Connor jumped down then strode up the path to the front door without being bidden. Louis and Luke followed him. A security light flared as they approached the house. No sooner had Connor stuck his key in the lock, a light went on in the hallway and the white UPVC door flung open.

A heavy-looking woman in a white fleece dressing gown with grey stars flared her nostrils angrily as she stared down at Connor, before standing aside to let him in. Her only words to him were, "Upstairs to bed."

Louis watched him thunder up the stairs then turned back to the foster carer. Before he could open his mouth to say anything, she launched into a hushed diatribe.

"Thanks for bringing him back, officers. I'm Becky, his carer. Has he made any allegations about me? He's been a little sod since day one of his placement, going missing all the time, playing up at school. I'll bet he's woken Maisie up now, that's my daughter.

She'll be grouchy at primary school tomorrow. Anyway, where did you find him?"

"City Square," replied Louis, who found himself taking a dislike to Becky the more she spoke. "And don't worry, he hasn't made any allegations against you."

"Well, that's good then," replied Becky, looking quite bored now. "What was he doing there? Has he been drinking? Drugs?"

"He doesn't smell of alcohol or weed," replied Luke. "He doesn't seem out of it, at any rate."

"Right," she said with a final nod. "Anyway, I'll have to get to bed. School run in the morning. If there's anything, you'll have to ring his social worker. Cheers, lads."

Without waiting, she closed the door.

Louis looked at Luke, who met his gaze with an amused chuckle. They walked towards the van, updating the control room on the way to confirm that Connor had been returned home.

CHAPTER 2

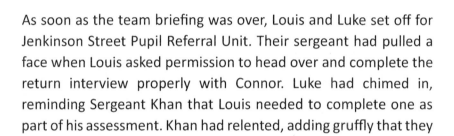

As soon as the team briefing was over, Louis and Luke set off for Jenkinson Street Pupil Referral Unit. Their sergeant had pulled a face when Louis asked permission to head over and complete the return interview properly with Connor. Luke had chimed in, reminding Sergeant Khan that Louis needed to complete one as part of his assessment. Khan had relented, adding gruffly that they should get it done as quickly as possible.

"So, how long do you give it before the kid tells us to fuck off?" asked Luke. "Under ten seconds, I bet."

"I'm feeling lucky," grinned Louis. "Minute and a half."

"Loser buys the coffees."

They pulled up in the visitors' car park of the school. Louis stepped out of the car and looked over at the foreboding building. He could see why it was nicknamed Jenkatraz. A tall, dark-green metal fence surrounded the old, grey stone building. The black clouds in the sky did little to make it appear any more inviting. Louis pondered on whether it might have been an old church at some point as he rang the buzzer on the front gate. He introduced himself to the receptionist, who buzzed them in.

They were led through a maze of dull corridors by a member of staff and deposited in a small classroom. Louis sat on one of the orange plastic chairs and looked around at the white walls. Bits of artwork were dotted around, interspersed with public health posters about drugs, knives and sex. Luke wandered round from wall to wall. He was pointing out a large fist-shaped indent in the plaster when the door opened and Connor was brought in by the same member of staff. She told him to take Louis and Luke back to reception when they had finished, then closed the door as she left.

Louis caught the slightest flicker of amusement playing on Connor's lips as he walked over and dropped down in a chair on the opposite side of the table to Louis. Today, Connor was wearing a pair of black Nike joggers and matching zip-up top. He looked somewhere between thin and lean. His blond curls were unruly and there were dark shadows under his brilliant blue eyes.

"Alright?" he grunted by way of a greeting, slouching in his chair and drumming his fingertips on the desk.

"Got you out of maths?" asked Louis.

Connor nodded, not making eye contact. Louis could see he was trying to hold back a smile. Luke had seated himself in a corner of the classroom and was tapping away at his handheld terminal, giving Louis space.

"Right then, let's talk about yesterday," Louis said. "What you were up to."

"Nowt," replied Connor. "Just chilling in town."

"By yourself at one in the morning?"

"Best way."

"Had something happened for you to go missing?"

14

"I wasn't missing," replied Connor, looking bored as he continued to drum his fingers. "Becky only reports me because she has to. It suits her for me to be out of the house. She gets paid either way."

Louis was a little taken aback by the kid's grim cynicism. "How long have you been with her?"

Connor shrugged. "About six months. She's my ninth placement so far."

"That's a lot of moves," replied Louis, Connor's use of the words 'so far' not escaping his notice. "I think my record was four."

Connor looked up, studied Louis intently for a moment then dropped his gaze again. "Care Order?"

"Section twenty," replied Louis, referring to the part of the Children Act 1989 that allowed for parents to voluntarily admit their children into the local authority's care. Connor's entry into the system had evidently been related to concerns of abuse or neglect, and more than likely contested by his parents. "My mum was poorly and there wasn't anyone to look after me. The social workers made her sign me over until she got better."

Connor shuffled uncomfortably in his chair. "Anyway, I didn't do anything wrong and no one did anything to me. That bloke I shoved was just being a div. He's a mate of mine."

"Seems a bit old to be your mate?"

"Better than some of the dickheads my own age," snorted Connor. "Honestly, he's not a nonce or anything. He's sound."

"What's his name, then? Let me make sure he's not going to cause you any problems."

"Dean Wilkinson," Connor replied with unexpected candour.

"Everyone calls him Wilko."

Louis glanced over at Luke, who met his gaze and nodded imperceptibly. Louis knew Luke would now be running the name through police systems via his handheld terminal. "So, if he's your mate, why were you so pissed off with him?"

Connor shrugged. "I'd given him someone money to buy us some tinnies and he'd drank them all."

"You were shouting at him about a woman, though?"

Connor looked up for a moment. "He said his bird was coming down with some more."

Louis snorted. "Seems a bit over the top for you to knock him on his arse, then. I don't buy it, pal."

"That's not my problem," Connor replied boredly. "Anyway, I'm fine. I won't do it again."

Louis studied the boy for a moment then said, "I hope not. You probably think you can take care of yourself but it can be dangerous out there."

Even as he said it, Louis cringed inwardly. He remembered professionals telling him the same thing and it hadn't made a jot of difference at the time. They were right, of course, but he had been too embroiled in his own problems to care.

"Whatever," murmured Connor, standing up. "Are we done? This is actually worse than maths."

"Yeah, we're done," Louis conceded.

Luke joined him and Connor led them to reception then vanished back into the grey labyrinth with a grunt that Louis took to mean goodbye. As they walked to the car, Luke reported his findings on

Wilko. "He's harmless enough. Just an alcoholic. You'll see him lingering at the traffic lights on the busier routes into the city trying to scrouge some pennies for the day's cider. No sex offences though."

"I wonder why they were together," mused Louis, opening the car door and sliding into the passenger seat. He didn't yet have his response permit, so Luke did the driving in case they had to expedite to an emergency call.

Luke got in and started the engine. "Get it scripted up. We can put a referral through to social services as well. Maybe they'll do a bit more digging with him."

Or not, thought Louis. Aloud, he said, "Sure. I can do it whilst I enjoy that coffee you're going to buy me. Not one F-bomb."

Luke laughed and set the car in motion, heading in the direction of the nearest coffee drive-thru.

* * * * *

Connor sat alone in the dark, vacant classroom, propping his head up in his hand. He felt exhausted. No sooner had he climbed into bed and closed his eyes, it was time to get up again. Becky had hammered loudly on his door at quarter-to-seven, telling him to get ready. Her six-year-old daughter Maisie was whinging loudly about something on the landing. Connor hadn't bothered to try and block out the noise, figuring he could at least get some sleep at school later.

The clock on the wall read half-past one. Half an hour until home time. With any luck, no one would notice he was gone and he could catch a quick nap here. Something to thank that nosy copper for, he supposed. Connor figured he must be new. The officer's light-brown skin had a fresh, healthy look and his dark eyes seemed to take everything in. The fact that he'd shared some personal information was unusual in itself. Connor had met plenty of cops in his time, some of whom had a deeply-ingrained weariness about them and a deadness behind their eyes; for the most part, they just wanted to do what needed to be done and then be on their way. The taller, handier-looking copper didn't have that look about him, but it was clear that he was the more experienced of the two. In any case, they were gone now and he could get his head down.

The door swung open and the lights clicked on. No such luck. Connor blinked under the bright fluorescent lights. A tall, athletic man stood in the doorway holding a piece of paper and a mug of what smelt like hot chocolate. He closed the door and came into the room. He was dressed in black Underarmour joggers and a white t-shirt of the same brand. His brown hair was styled into a neat quiff. Connor's nose wrinkled at the scent of whatever expensive aftershave he was wearing. Mr Penton sat down in the chair that had been occupied by Louis ten minutes ago and slapped a sheet of paper down in front of Connor.

Connor saw a dozen mathematical problems on the paper and rolled his eyes.

"I'm sure you weren't trying to get out of maths, Connor," Mr Penton said cheerfully, flashing a smile worthy of a Hollywood movie star. He pushed the mug of hot chocolate across the table towards Connor, who cupped it in his hands and took a sip.

"Sorry, Elliott," said Connor, knowing the teacher would chide him for referring to him as Mr Penton. He yawned and stretched. "I was tired."

"So I see," replied Elliott. "Come on, get cracking with these. We can stay here while you do them."

Connor took the pen that Elliott handed him and began looking at the problems.

"What did the police want?"

"Asking me what I was doing last night," replied Connor, filling in the answer to the first problem. He was actually quite good at maths and these problems weren't particularly taxing. Even so, he deliberately worked on them slowly.

"You were out? Any luck?"

Connor looked up, noted Elliott's concerned expression then shook his head and went back to the worksheet.

"Too bad. I thought we talked about being out so late though. You'll get into trouble."

"I know," replied Connor, filling in another answer. "Wilko reckoned she'd be coming down to City Square. We waited for ages and then the cops came."

"Did you give him money?"

"A fiver to buy some cider."

"Hmm. You've got to be careful, Connor. Those kinds of people will tell you whatever they think you want to hear if it'll get them another fix of their drug of choice."

Connor shrugged. He knew Elliott was right. You couldn't trust anyone, really. Although, he had felt pretty confident that Wilko had been telling the truth.

"Did Becky give you a hard time?"

Connor nodded.

"I'm sure I'll hear all about it in your next review meeting. Aliyah's just sent the invites out."

"What's the point of being a teacher when all you do is go to meetings?" grumbled Connor, slapping the pen down onto the paper and sliding the completed worksheet back to Elliott. Aliyah had been his social worker ever since he had come into care. It seemed like there was a meeting about him every five minutes and the thought of everyone sitting around a table bitching about him was infuriating. Elliott, his keyworker at school, would always attend the meetings and feed back the discussions. It would particularly aggravate Connor to hear that Becky would complain about him. How could she moan about his bad behaviour when most of the time he wasn't there.

"Well, I don't mind," replied Elliott cheerfully as he scanned the worksheet and ticked all twelve problems. "They may call you an antisocial little twerp, but at least I can remind them that you're actually quite intelligent."

Connor sat back in his chair, crossed his arms and huffed. "That copper was in care."

"Oh really?"

Connor nodded. "As if he actually turned up here though! I was just taking the piss when I told him to."

Elliott shrugged. "That's the police for you. No sense of humour."

"He was alright," Connor replied, yawning loudly. "Not like some of them."

Elliott's tone was suddenly grave, causing Connor to look up. "All the same, the less you have to do with them, the better."

"Yeah, okay." Connor dropped his gaze away from Elliott's green eyes. Just occasionally, the sparkling movie-star charm would give way to a darker, more intense expression.

"Come on," said Elliott, standing up. "You can go early."

Connor sprang to his feet and followed Elliott. As they reached the door, Elliott turned and put his hand on Connor's shoulder. "Promise me, straight home today and no late-night outings."

Connor nodded emphatically. Elliott waited a moment then, seemingly satisfied that his instruction had been taken on board, let go of Connor's shoulder. They went via the locker room for Connor to collect his bag and jacket then Elliott signed him out and walked him to the gate.

"See you tomorrow, Connor," said Elliott, tapping his access card against the sensor to release the gate.

Connor nodded and stepped out onto the pavement. The gate closed with a metallic clang. As he began walking away from the school, Connor looked over his shoulder and saw Elliott still watching him. "I know, straight home!"

Within a few moments, the school was out of sight. He found himself walking toward the Woodfield Estate, a large cluster of red-brick council houses. The sharp wintery breeze stabbed at his chest and torso, causing him to gasp. He zipped his jacket up, for all the good it did. He was within the estate now, the familiar streets looking smaller and shabbier somehow. Not that they had been particularly large or grand when he had lived there.

He rounded a corner onto Woodfield Crescent. Number twelve was in darkness. He paused for a moment, staring at the weary-looking house. One of the living room windows was boarded up and the garden hadn't seen a lawnmower in some time. This had been home once. Connor sighed heavily. A black Ford Focus rumbled passed suddenly and turned into the driveway, breaking him out of his thoughts. A woman and two children alighted from the car, the two kids scrabbling for position as the woman reached inside her handbag for the keys. Connor turned and carried on walking.

The parade of shops beckoned him with neon lights. The chip-shop, Chinese and pizza takeaways were closed. At this time of day, only the convenience store was open. He stepped inside, glad for the rush of warmth from the heaters and the strange, sweet smell of incense. He helped himself to a can of Red Bull then went to pay. The Indian lady behind the counter said hello as he put the coins down. She handed him a little white paper bag and smiled kindly.

"Cheers," said Connor, returning her smile. He picked up his goods and left the store. The lady didn't speak much English, or so he thought. He had once intervened when her son was being picked on outside the shop by some local bullies. If there was something he hated more than bullies, it was racists. Connor had smashed one of them in the face with his fist, causing them to scurry off and leave the boy in peace. Ever since then, the lady always gave him a little bag of penny sweets when she served him.

Connor made his way to the grassed play area nearby. The usual playground furniture was surrounded by dark green railings. He chose to sit atop one of the metal benches rather than go into the play area. It was nearly home time and the kids from the local primary school would swarm here any minute. He opened his drink and took a few swallows, gasping as the cold liquid made his chest clench. He dug into the white paper bag and smiled when he saw cola cubes – his favourite. He popped one in his mouth and stuffed the bag into his pocket.

A siren rang out in the distance. An ambulance maybe, or the police. Always some drama around here, he thought to himself. Woodfield wasn't the worst estate to live on, but it wasn't without its problems. He'd opened the door to the police plenty of times as a kid, usually after something had happened to Emma.

Connor thought about the copper who'd spoken to him today. He'd been alright, as cops go. Unusual to see a professional who actually did what they'd agreed to do. Apart from Elliott, Connor couldn't think of anyone from his so-called Core Group of professionals that he could particularly rely on.

Connor reached into his pocket when he felt his mobile phone buzz. A text message from Becky telling him not to be late home; Aliyah was coming to see him. His first instinct was to send a shrugging emoji. Making small talk with his social worker was something he couldn't be bothered to do right now. Then he remembered his promise to Elliott. With a heavy sigh, he sent a thumbs-up emoji, hopped off the bench and began a slow trudge back to Becky's house.

CHAPTER 3

Connor tried the front door and walked in. He'd spotted Aliyah's beige Mini Cooper parked outside as he reached the driveway. He followed the sound of the two female voices into the living room.

Becky and Aliyah were sat on the large grey corner-group sofa. Aliyah was a slender young Asian woman, dressed stylishly in skinny black jeans, a black blazer and black Converse trainers. Her dark hair was tied up in an elaborate bun. By comparison, Becky looked like a life-sized Peppa Pig in her bright pink tracksuit set.

Connor dropped himself heavily onto the grey footstool in the opposite corner and waited to be addressed. He hated this room. He'd hated it from the day Aliyah had brought him here. The walls were painted grey, the carpets were grey. The only splashes of colour were from the white fluffy rugs and cushions, along with the tacky chandelier. Becky with so proud of this room.

"Alright, Connor?" Aliyah beamed in his direction, her broad Yorkshire accent at total odds with her exotic beauty.

"Alright," he replied nonchalantly. As social workers went, he didn't mind Aliyah. She came to see him more regularly than she needed to and seemed to take a genuine interest in how he was doing. There was something up, though. Becky sat stiffly on the sofa, eyes flitting to various points in the room. Aliyah hadn't drawn her notebook out of her oversized Louis Vuitton handbag yet.

"Becky's been telling me you were out late last night," said Aliyah. "What've you been up to now?"

Connor shrugged.

"The police report says that they found you hanging round in town near The Plum with a man?"

Connor stretched and yawned. "I already told them. Nothing happened."

"Yes, but it's dangerous, Connor. Mr Penton's only just covered child sexual exploitation with you."

"I wasn't selling my arse, idiot!" he snapped.

"Connor!" hissed Becky. She hated him swearing in Maisie's earshot. No doubt, the little brat would be lurking on the landing trying to eavesdrop.

Connor folded his arms. "You lot don't know what you're on about."

Aliyah cleared her throat and continued. "Anyway, Becky and I have been talking. You've been going missing more and more. You're obviously putting yourself at risk when you're out.

Connor rolled his eyes.

"It's really disruptive, Connor." Becky chimed in. "Maisie's had a bad day at school today because she got woken up by the police bringing you home at stupid o'clock this morning. Mickey's knackered as well. It's not good for him to be driving to work on the motorway like that. Anyway, I'm going to have to give notice on you."

Connor's head snapped up at that remark. Becky was ending his placement. Aliyah had twenty-eight days to find him somewhere else. He caught Aliyah shooting Becky an irritated sideways glance. Aliyah was many things, but she wasn't insensitive. Connor could feel his cheeks getting hotter. He didn't give a shit if Becky wanted him out. That was absolutely fine. It was just.... what if they had to move him way out? He wouldn't be at Jenkatraz anymore. What if it was harder to get to City Square. He might never see...

"Ah, get fucked!" Connor leapt to his feet and stormed out of the house, slamming the front door hard as he left. He stomped down the drive and ran for a little while until he was far enough away from the house. He pulled his phone out to check the time. Nearly four o'clock. They'd be leaving him to cool off for now. Aliyah would probably try to ring and text him around five before she finished work. Becky would make the prerequisite calls and texts on the hour until nine o'clock. At ten, she'd send him a text warning him to come home or she'd be reporting him missing. She'd call the police shortly after that, put the report in then take herself off to bed. That gave him a few hours yet.

It was already getting darker and colder. Connor shivered, wishing he'd grabbed a thicker jacket. He tossed another cola cube into his mouth and stood in the shadows near the bus stop. The last thing he needed was for Aliyah to spot him if she drove past. Mercifully, he didn't have long to wait. The glow of an approaching bus appeared in the distance. Connor waited until the last minute then stepped forward and signalled to it. The driver nodded as Connor flashed his pass. He sat at the back of the virtually-empty bus with his hood up. It would be twenty minutes or so before it reached the city centre.

* * * * *

27

Louis poked at his petrol-station pasta salad boredly as he gazed at the large LCD television mounted on the wall of the break room in Weaver's Yard Police Station. The imposing six-storey building towered above the surrounding warehouses on the edge of the city. It was coming up seven o'clock so Luke had brought them back in to meal. Luke was laid out on the battered blue couch, his body-armour and tac-vest on the floor beside him.

It had been quiet for a Thursday night. Louis had quickly learned that there was no rhyme or reason to the busyness of a shift: he had worked some Saturday nights with nothing more taxing than a few drunken scraps that needed breaking up, and some Tuesday daytimes where all hell had broken loose. Luke had taught him to enjoy the downtime whenever it came.

"Sixty quid for a pair of dancing shoes!" Luke suddenly exclaimed, phone in hand.

"Didn't think they'd make them in your size, pal," chuckled Louis.

"Knobhead," Luke replied, grinning. "Our lass telling me that's how much for Evie's new dancing shoes. Best sign myself up for some football overtime before I book off tonight."

Louis smiled. Luke always had a tale to tell about his wife's extravagant spending on their two young daughters. Louis suspected that it was probably Luke that spoiled them rotten. Those kids were his pride and joy. He had no doubt Evie would get her shoes.

The door swung open and two officers walked in, brown paper McDonalds bags in hand. Damien Haley stood slightly taller than Luke at six foot four with tattoo sleeves down both his long, muscular arms. There could be no doubt that he was a regular at the gym. He was brutishly handsome – thick blond hair, a five o-clock shadow that emphasised his hollow cheeks and a pair of cold, blue eyes. His Glaswegian accent seemed to suit his brooding manner perfectly. He slid his massive frame effortlessly into a chair at the table next to Louis', barely acknowledging him. His partner was quite the opposite.

"Lovely Louis!" exclaimed Sharlene Davey, wrapping her arms round Louis' neck from behind and kissing his right cheek before sitting down next to him.

Louis greeted her with a bashful grin, suddenly feeling self-conscious. "Alright, Sharlene."

Sharlene was almost as tall as Damien and Luke with smooth black skin and long braids tied up into a messy bun at the back of her head. Her parents had emigrated from Jamaica to the UK in the seventies. Beautiful and brash, she had squealed with delight when she learnt that Louis was part Creole on his father's side during their first shift together guarding an abandoned cannabis factory.

"Yuh irie, Lukas?" she called over to Luke, switching from her broad local accent to thick patois as she reached out to high-five him.

"Mi irie," Luke called back, reaching his hand over his head and slapping her palm. "Go on, Sharl, do us some chips."

Sharlene dug into her bag, fished out some chips and lowered them into Luke's mouth. He chomped down on them, mumbling gratefully.

Louis grinned. He'd been fortunate to land on a well-established team with a nice mix of personalities and experience. Some of his training cohort hadn't been so lucky. Sharlene, Luke and Damien were the most experienced on the team, save for Sergeant Khan.

Compared to Luke and Sharlene, Damien was gruff and sullen for the most part. Louis had wondered if it was something personal at first until Luke reassured him that it wasn't. Even now, Damien was responding to Luke's questions about football overtime with practically one-word answers.

Meanwhile, Sharlene chatted away to Louis, munching her cheeseburger and pushing her fries towards him to share. "So, what have you been up to tonight, darling? Nearly signed off?"

"Nearly," replied Louis, helping himself to a couple of fries. "Missing person return interview done now. Not much left to go."

"Good lad! And how's that gorgeous hunk of yours?"

Louis blushed when he saw both Luke and Damien look over at him. "He's fine."

Sharlene glared at her two colleagues and exclaimed, "His cat, dickheads!"

Suddenly, all four of their radios crackled to life with the same message. "Control, anyone free to take me a juvenile high risk misper? Reported today at 18:30 from Fir Tree Gardens."

Connor, Louis thought to himself when he heard the address. He looked over to Luke, who had clearly had the same idea. Luke swung his legs off the couch onto the floor and picked up his radio. "One-nine, show us on it. Let one-seven finish their meal."

"Cheers, darling," said Sharlene, blowing Luke a kiss.

Louis stood up and received a nod of acknowledgement from Damien. He waited for Luke to finish pulling on his kit then they headed to the stairs.

"Like bloody Groundhog Day, isn't it," grumbled Luke, unsnapping the car-key from the carabiner on his tac-vest.

"It's his social worker who's rung it in," said Louis, reading the log from his handheld terminal. "She's asking for a call."

They got into the car. While Louis began dialling the phone number on the log, Luke contacted the control room to say that they'd head to City Square first to see if they could spot Connor.

A woman answered Louis' call after the third ring and he introduced himself. She thanked him for calling back and proceeded to explain the events of that afternoon. Louis pinched the bridge of his nose as he listened. Another broken-down placement.

"Any idea why he's hanging around City Square?" he asked.

"Not a clue," replied Aliyah. "I asked him tonight and the best I got was that he wasn't selling his arse."

"Any other ideas on where he might go? Any family or friends?"

Louis listened intently and jotted some details in his pocket notebook as Aliyah gave him a potted version of Connor's last few years.

"So, in a nutshell," Aliyah concluded, "He could be anywhere."

"Okay," replied Louis. "We're going to start at City Square. We're on until 1am but the Shift Commander's graded Connor as high risk, so they'll keep units on him until he's found."

"Thanks," replied Aliyah. "When you find him, do me a favour and drop me a text whatever the time."

Louis agreed that he would and ended the call, pleasantly surprised that Aliyah seemed a little more bothered about Connor than his foster carer. He fed back what he had learned from her to

Luke, who listened as he drove.

"Something about this kid seems to be pushing your buttons."

Louis trusted Luke enough to answer him truthfully. "A little. I spent some time in care when my mum was sectioned."

He paused, half expecting a speech about not getting too involved, but none came. "I was lucky, I suppose. Eventually, they let her out and helped her get set up again so I could go home to her. This kid's got no-one."

Luke nodded gravely. "We'll find him. Here, try and ring him, see if he picks up."

Simple but effective, Louis supposed. He referred to his notebook and dialled the number Aliyah had given him for Connor. He was surprised when it started ringing rather than going to voicemail. He was just about to hang up when Connor's voice came on the line. "Who's this?"

"Police," replied Louis instinctively, before catching himself. "It's Louis. I came to see you at school."

To his surprise, the line didn't go dead. "Oh yeah. What's up, Louis?"

Louis turned to Luke, who could hear the conversation and was clearly amused by Connor's cheek. "Pretty sure you said you weren't going to do this again?"

"Yeah, well, shit happens."

"Where are you?"

"I'm fine, mate, honest," Connor said brightly. Wherever he was, he was outside. "I'll be home on the next bus."

"No, you won't," Louis replied. "Come on, Connor, people are worried about you."

"There's no need."

Louis gave an exasperated sigh. He remembered that tone of voice. There'd be no persuading Connor to go back to Becky's until he was good and ready. "Do what you need to do, Connor, but we're still going to look for you."

"Fine."

"Be honest with me though, have you got your inhaler?"

A short silence. "Yeah."

"Alright. Try and go somewhere warm, at least, you little prat." The barb was delivered with good humour and evidently received in the spirit it was intended.

"Good luck, copper!"

The line went dead.

* * * * *

Bryan Hillesley dropped down into his padded black computer chair and sipped his fresh mug of coffee. He smacked his thick lips as the sour liquid made its way down his throat. From behind his thin, rectangular glasses, his eyes darted left to right as he scanned the private chat window for new text from his friend.

Maybe 'friend' was too generous a term, mused Bryan as he read what 'blueeyedboi14' had written.

"SO COLD."

"WISH I COULD BE SOMEWHERE WARM."

Bryan typed back, "My place is nice and warm. Having a hot coffee too."

"Nice. You should invite me."

Bryan grinned. "You'd only run off like last time."

"Promise I won't this time."

"Doesn't matter." Bryan manoeuvred his mouse and, after a few deft clicks, an image popped into the chat window. A door with several deadbolts and locks on it.

"I guess no escape," came blueeyedboi14's response followed by a laughing emoji.

"No escape," he typed back.

"You'd be able to do anything."

Bryan shifted in his chair, readjusting the crotch of his grey joggers. When he next looked, a computer-generated image had appeared in the chat window. A blue-eyed teenager with curly blond hair looking terrified at some unseen danger.

The chat window pinged multiple times with more computer-generated images of the same teenager, distressed in each one. He leaned forward and hovered his mouse over the one that particularly took his fancy. A large hand was wrapped tight around the lad's throat, strangling him. The bright blue eyes were glassy, eyelids drooping.

Bryan licked his lips. Delicious. "Would you let me do that?"

"Yeh. Anything to be somewhere warm for the night."

CHAPTER 4

Louis climbed wearily into his bed and stretched out across the king-sized mattress, letting a deep sigh of relief escape him. His bedroom was deliberately simple: a bed and two wooden side tables and a chest of drawers that contrasted the light mocha walls. He kept most of his clothes in a wardrobe in the spare bedroom along with a single bed for the occasional guest. Downstairs was an open-plan living room with a breakfast bar separating the kitchen. French doors opened into a modest back yard with wooden fencing that unfortunately hid the view of the field behind it. There had been plans to build more houses, but apparently the developers had run out of money. Even so, it was a nice house on a new-build estate away from the city.

Louis curled his toes under the quilt and smiled, grateful for home. He had never anticipated being able to afford his own place. After joining the police, he had decided to be brave and apply for a mortgage. The results were pleasantly surprising. He had moved in here eight months ago but was still in awe of having his own space.

As if on cue, he heard a hurried padding from the hallway into the bedroom. A dark shape leapt from the floor onto the foot of the bed and made its way to Louis' chest. Gonzo was a large tabby with a long, luxurious coat. Named after Louis' favourite Muppets character, Gonzo was a rescue; although Louis often wondered who had rescued who. The shelter worker mooted that he was part Norwegian Forest cat, hence his powerful build and thick fur. Green, intelligent eyes blinked gently at Louis, who scratched the purring feline's head between his velveteen ears.

His phone screen lit up and he reached over to check it. The time was two-thirty in the morning. Despite best efforts, he and Luke had not been able to find Connor. Due to Connor's age and being graded high-risk, CID had taken over. They had briefed the two night-detectives before retiring from duty. The message was from a dating app Louis was signed up to. He didn't bother to read whether it was someone sending a personal message to him or just some spam, too tired and strung out to care.

He placed his phone back on the bedside table and turned it over so he wouldn't be disturbed by its glow again. Louis had never been the best sleeper, so working shifts was doing him no favours in that regard. He twisted over onto his left side, dislodging Gonzo from atop his chest. There were no hard feelings. Gonzo stretched out next to Louis, his head just below the pillow and his white front paws kneading the duvet gently.

Louis stroked Gonzo slowly, pondering the last couple of days. Luke had been right to point out that Connor's situation was pushing Louis' buttons. Of course, Connor's circumstances were very different to his own but they took him back to his own adolescence all the same. A lack of control that came with a group of so-called professionals making decisions about his life. Writing down everything he did or said. The way other kids and teachers looked at him in school now that he was suddenly a Looked After Child, or 'LAC' for short, as he would hear professionals say. Lacking something. Louis closed his eyes and tried to slow his breathing down.

As an adult, Louis could acknowledge that the four sets of foster carers he'd had were ok. They'd looked after him as well as anyone could have looked after a twelve-year old mixed-race boy from one of the rougher inner-city estates, whose moods mainly swung from sullen to angry. There was still an indifference, though, that Louis had constantly sensed. A feeling that, if he were moved on, some other kid would take his place and he'd be forgotten about. His presence would have made no impact whatsoever. Louis had picked that up from the few moments he'd spent with Connor's foster carer. He got no sense from his first impression that she was particularly interested in nurturing the vulnerable children placed with her.

Nurturing. Louis pondered on that word for a moment, looking down at Gonzo's purring form as he did so. It was something he constantly looked for and valued in other people. He thought of Luke, who coached children's rugby in his spare time, and Sharlene's constant fundraising efforts for community charities. Good people.

The train of thought arrived at Damien. Cold, intense, brooding. As far from nurturing as Louis could imagine. An axe-wielding Viking might be less scary. Louis shivered at the thought, picturing Damien's powerful arms and steely-blue eyes. He chided himself for the uncharitable thought. After finishing his meal, Damien's inimitable Glaswegian accent had come over the radio to say that he and Sharlene would assist in searching for Connor as well.

Connor, Louis thought grimly. He used his finger to lift up his phone enough to peek at the screen. No updates. Exhaling heavily, he settled back down and closed his eyes.

* * * * *

Connor leaned against Jenkatraz' fence and rubbed his shoulders, trying in vain to warm up. Just before his phone had finally died, the time had been six-thirty in the morning. He had made his way to the school even though he knew it would be locked up tight for the time being. He was freezing cold. The January night had been clear and chilly, but mercifully dry.

The scrape of tyres on gravel made Connor look up. A red Audi had just pulled up in the staff car park. Connor watched Elliott alight from the car and fish out a black leather gym-bag from the back seat. In spite of the weather, he was wearing shorts. The staff were allowed to use the school's gym equipment for free and Connor recalled Elliott telling him that he often had a quick workout before pupils arrived.

Connor had pondered arriving at the normal school time but the likelihood of another teacher spotting his dishevelled state and making a major incident out of it was high. Elliott would do his safeguarding duty but he would at least do it in a low-key way. Aside from that, Connor wasn't sure he could hold out another hour in this freezing cold air.

Gritting his teeth, he tried to steady himself so he wouldn't sound too cold when he spoke. He walked towards the front gate, timing his arrival with Elliott's.

"Connor!" Elliott did not look impressed.

"Alright." Connor smiled weakly, unable to stop his teeth chattering.

"Look at the state of you! Have you been out all night?" Elliott opened the gate with his key card and ushered Connor in.

Connor breathed a sigh of relief when they entered the school reception. The air was warm, thanks to the central heating. The cleaners had finished for the morning but the odour of pine disinfectant lingered. Elliott opened the door to a chill-out room, which Connor referred to as the padded cell. Softly-lit with various large beanbags, blankets and little else, it was supposed to be for pupils who needed time out, or who were otherwise having a meltdown.

Connor threw himself down into the largest blue beanbag and pulled a couple of blankets over him. Elliott disappeared for a few minutes then returned with a hot water bottle, a mug of hot chocolate and a Frosties bar. Connor accepted all three from him gratefully.

"I thought we agreed you were going to stay put for the night," said Elliott, seating himself cross-legged on the floor.

"Shit happens," muttered Connor, tearing into the Frosties bar and devouring it.

"Don't give me that." Elliott's voice had an edge this time.

Connor looked up. Elliott's green eyes had darkened and his jaw was tensed. "Becky's given notice on my placement. Aliyah came round last night and they told me then."

Elliott's expression softened. He produced another Frosties bar from the pocket of his dark-blue Nike hoody and handed it to Connor. "I'm sorry. Do you know where you're moving to?"

Connor shook his head. "What if they move me out of authority? I won't be able to find her!"

"There's a chance she might not want you to," Elliott replied gently.

Connor felt his eyes prickle. If it had been anybody else, he would have punched them.

"You've got to think carefully, Connor," Elliott continued. "The more you do this, the more likely you are to get shipped out. That's if you don't end up dead first."

Connor flinched when Elliott reached forward and touched his chin with his fingertips, moving his head to the right. "What's happened there?"

He was staring at two linear abrasions on Connor's neck, made all the more-livid by his pale skin.

"Dunno," snapped Connor, standing up and pacing round the room. He paused for a moment, gently kicking at a beanbag with his right foot as he gathered his thoughts. "She's my mum. All you professionals think she's a piece of shit and she doesn't care about me because she doesn't turn up to contact. She's not well! How's she supposed to remember one day every three months?"

"I don't know, Connor," replied Elliott with a heavy sigh. "If you were my kid, I'd like to think that I'd try."

Connor cocked his head in Elliott's direction. It occurred to him that he didn't know if Elliott had a family. "Do you have kids?"

Elliott shook his head. "Maybe I could find out where she is now?"

"You said Aliyah didn't know?" Connor flopped back onto the beanbags. He'd asked Aliyah plenty of times about where his mum was. Every time, Aliyah said she'd had no contact. She'd remind Connor that Emma was only allowed to see him four times a year because of her chaotic lifestyle. Once she settled down, she'd perhaps be allowed more time.

Aliyah must know where to find her, Connor had convinced himself. Even if Emma had forgotten what dates she was due to have contact, it would be easy enough for her to go to Aliyah's office and ask for them again. Maybe that was it. Emma had gone to the office, carried on with Aliyah and Aliyah hadn't given her the dates.

Connor caught himself. He wasn't a stupid kid anymore and this wasn't some fairytale. Emma was fucked off her face somewhere, cycling between crack and heroin. The courts weren't supposed to send women with kids to prison, but maybe she'd been caught nicking from Primark one too many times and the judge figured a spell inside was justified now that she didn't have him with her anymore.

His train of thought was interrupted by Elliott standing up. "Put your head down for a bit. I'll come get you at nine so you can go to your first lesson."

Connor nodded and waited for Elliott to close the door before curling up in a foetal position amongst the beanbags. The lights were still on but dim enough not to keep him awake. He yawned loudly, suddenly realising just how exhausted he was.

* * * * *

It was nearly ten-thirty when Louis awoke. He'd slept unusually heavily but didn't feel refreshed for it. After a coffee, a swift five-kilometre run along the nearby canal towpath and a hot shower, he felt better. Now sat on his sofa eating his staple breakfast of porridge with blueberries, the question of whether Connor had been found yet returned to niggle him as it had done since he had woken up.

He reached over to his work bag and pulled out his handheld terminal. As he switched the device on, Louis pondered whether he was getting too involved. Aliyah's number was still saved in his recent calls so he tapped it to dial out. She answered after a couple of rings, sounding stressed.

"He's back! Little sod showed up at school this morning. Elliott Penton, his keyworker, rang your lot earlier to tell them."

"That's great," replied Louis, feeling relieved. "Is he ok."

"Cold and hungry but otherwise ok. Well, actually..." Aliyah hesitated. "Elliott isn't sure, but he wonders if someone assaulted Connor. He looks like he's got some bruising around his neck, as if someone grabbed him. Mind you, I'd cheerfully throttle him at the moment!"

Louis chuckled. "Understandable. What happens to him now?"

"I'm in the middle of trying to find him a new placement," replied Aliyah. "It won't be easy. Not many people are interested in taking on a kid like Connor with so many placement breakdowns. Becky's obliged to keep him for twenty-eight days but frankly I want him out of there as soon as possible so he's got less of an excuse to do another runner."

"Let me know if there's anything I can do," said Louis, not actually sure whether there was.

"As it happens, we're holding a placement disruption meeting for him later this afternoon. It's virtual but I can send you the link. Would you be able to attend?"

"I guess so. I've never been to one before. What would you need me to do?"

"Nothing much," replied Aliyah. "There'll be a few different services there. My manager will chair it, but we'll be updating everyone with what's happened and looking at next steps. You'll get to meet some of the professionals working with him too. To be honest, apart from myself and Elliott, you're the only one to have taken any interest in Connor."

Louis heard the chime to say that the meeting link from Aliyah had arrived in his e-mail. She thanked him for agreeing to come and they ended the call. It would be a few hours yet before the meeting. Louis picked up his personal mobile phone and sent a text to Luke telling him the latest. Luke responded quickly. The meeting would sign off the multi-agency working element of Louis' final assessment, so it would make sense to do it. Even though they weren't due to start their shift until six that evening, Luke would square it with Sergeant Khan.

Louis hated the half-night shift, which started at six in the evening and finished at four in the morning. Full nights made more sense to his already haywire body-clock. A ten o'clock start and a seven o'clock finish. Not that it mattered at the moment, he thought grimly as he started out of the French doors at the grey, cloudy sky. Another couple of hours and it would be dark. He stretched out on the sofa, pulled a heavy brown throw over himself and switched the television for some background noise as he closed his eyes.

CHAPTER 5

The meeting started promptly enough at half-past one. Louis felt a little self-conscious of the fact that he was dialling in via his handheld terminal from his breakfast bar, the only place downstairs that could afford him a plain background. Most of the people, he noted, were probably in the same boat as him but had the facility of creating a false backdrop. Luke had somehow managed to generate a very professional-looking background with the force's corporate logo. Louis made a mental note to ask him how to do that.

He felt depressingly unsurprised to see Aliyah's earlier comment about very few people being interested in Connor's current situation borne out in the meeting attendance. Aside from Luke and Aliyah, the only people present were Aliyah's Team Manager Martin Boyd and a bored-looking school nurse called Heather Harper.

A notification popped up on screen to say Elliott Penton was in the waiting room. A moment later, his face joined the other five tiles. As Martin called the meeting to order, Louis studied Elliott. Handsome like a model, dark green eyes and thick brown hair styled up in a quiff. He and Aliyah clearly knew each other well as they exchanged greetings and laughed about something to do with Love Island. Elliott's voice was deep but warm, reassuring.

His attention snapped back into the meeting as he heard Martin call his name, awaiting an introduction. "PC Louis Mortimer, Patrol Team 5."

The meeting started in earnest with Aliyah outlining the current situation for Connor. She gave apologies from Becky in a tone of voice that left Louis in no doubt at all that she wasn't impressed with the foster carer. The placement had broken down irrevocably so Connor would have to be moved. The news had prompted him to go missing overnight, his second episode in as many days.

At that point, Heather had piped up that she had another meeting to dial into and passed over that Connor was due an asthma clinic review. When he was in his new placement, let her know and she would make arrangements for him. With that, she was gone.

Louis heard his mobile phone ping and looked down to see a message from Luke – a female runner emoji. Louis stifled a grin and replied with a shrugging emoji and a laughing face.

Aliyah went on to say that there were no suitable in-house foster carers suitable for Connor, and authorisation hadn't been given to seek an external placement. Louis felt a pang of disappointment at the thought that there were people making a business out of looking after vulnerable children.

"So," continued Aliyah, "We've decided to place Connor at Robin Hill Children's Home. Two of their residents have just moved into independent accommodation so he'll be living there with only two other children initially. He'll more than likely benefit from the extra staff attention. My hope is that the group-home environment will be less pressured than having to fit in with a foster family."

Louis knew of Robin Hill. Unlike other children's homes in the area, this one had been purpose-built on some council-owned land in one of the more affluent parts of the district. The private residents in the surrounding area had argued hard for the home not to be built but had lost out. Louis had been out to many a report regarding nuisance youths carrying on and smoking cannabis. For the most part, it had been a couple of teenagers stood near the home's gate listening to music on a mobile phone, drinking nothing stronger than Pepsi Max and smoking cheap roll-ups.

Elliott spoke up next. "He should be able to get the bus to school easily enough. If it helps, I can offer some home visits to keep him on top of his curriculum and settle him."

"Thanks Elliott, that would be helpful," said Aliyah. "Louis, I'm mindful that Connor hasn't had a return interview since coming back this morning. We thought it would be best for him to carry on with his school day and try later. I don't suppose that's something you can help with?"

Louis wasn't sure how to answer. Of course, he would be happy to do it but he didn't want to promise something then let people down. It was a relief when Elliott spoke up.

"I talked to Connor at length this morning. Basically, he just roamed the streets by himself."

"All the same, I'd prefer for him to be seen by the police," Aliyah replied firmly. "I'm still a little concerned about those marks on his neck that you mentioned."

Martin chimed in, echoing Aliyah's concern.

"Leave it with us," Luke said. "Louis and I are on shift from six tonight. When is he landing at Robin Hill?"

"I'm collecting him from school to take him straight there," replied Aliyah. "I'll go via Becky's to collect his things, not that there's much to collect. I'll stay with him until you arrive. With any luck, he won't do a runner."

Louis gritted his teeth, feeling a hotness in his cheeks as he remembered packing four bin-bags of his worldly possessions into his social worker's car.

Elliott spoke up again. "There's just one thing, Aliyah. Where are things at with his contact with Emma? It must be nearly six months now since he last saw her. I know that has really been playing on Connor's mind."

"I know," replied Aliyah. "The problem is, she's lost her tenancy and she's not in any temporary accommodation currently, as far as I'm aware. When she was evicted from her council property, there was no statutory duty to rehouse her."

"She can't have just vanished though?"

Louis wasn't sure if Aliyah leaned in deliberately to emphasise her point but her tone was direct. "Believe me, Elliott, I've done everything I can to try and locate her. She's no longer on an order to Probation, she's definitely not in the prison system and she's not attending the Women's Centre anymore. If you have any ideas, I'm open to them."

"It's difficult, isn't it, "Elliott conceded. "But there must be some service working with her? Wasn't she attending the drugs project for her methadone script?"

Whilst Elliott and Aliyah carried on their exchange, Louis sent a message to Luke. Do we know her?

He watched Luke's head shift position on the screen, apparently bringing up a new window and studying the information on it. After a moment, he broke in. "Emma McAllen. No recent arrests but plenty of intelligence on her. Neighbourhood Policing are sighting her pretty regularly on Garnett Street."

It was Martin who spoke next. "Apologies, everyone, but you can probably tell from my accent that I'm not from round here. Garnett Street?

"The city's red-light area," replied Luke. "It's on the edge of the city-centre. Technically, it's residential but in practice it's all multi-occupancy bedsits and temporary accommodation. A lot of commuters use it as a cut-through into the city-centre, which the working girls and their punters alike find useful. There's quite a few disused mill buildings and warehouses nearby to go and do business in. Actually, there's a fair bit of concern for Emma. She's lost a lot of weight and bang at it with heroin and crack. No fixed abode. She refuses to engage with street outreach unless it's to grab clean needles."

"That explains a lot," Aliya replied gravely. "She's really spiralling. It probably wouldn't be good for Connor to see her in that state."

"It can't be any worse than what he's making up in his head," said Elliott. "Is there anything the police can do to help her?"

Louis shifted uncomfortably in his seat. Those deep green eyes seemed to be boring into him. "I guess we could speak to Neighbourhoods and see if they can make contact with her, find out where she's living?"

He felt pleased when he saw Elliott give a satisfied nod of thanks. Elliott was right in what he was saying. Louis remembered the months he had spent trying to block out images of where his mum was. They told him that she was in a hospital, which made him picture her full of tubes and monitors, unable to speak to him. The couple of times when they spoke on the phone, she sounded distant and flat to the extent that Louis had been sure that someone was impersonating her just to try and fool him into thinking she was alive. It was reassuring to think that Connor had someone like Elliott in his corner.

The meeting ended shortly afterwards with Martin and Aliyah thanking everyone for their attendance. Louis ended the call on his handheld terminal then looked at his personal mobile. In his contacts book, he scrolled to the record named Rona. His thumb hovered over the call icon, then to the text icon. He hesitated for a moment then put the phone down on the worktop. He needed to get showered and ready for work.

* * * * *

Louis looked out of the patrol car into the drizzly gloom that surrounded Robin Hill Children's Home whilst Luke manoeuvred into a parking bay. The sandstone-coloured building looked out of place on the hill by itself. Just along the bend of the main road lay a village full of expensive Victorian houses, the occupants of which were greatly resentful to have such a stark representation of society's problems on their doorsteps.

Louis got out of the car and walked with Luke across the car park to the front door, a large double-glazed panel set in a grey steel frame. He noticed a red Audi and a beige Mini Cooper parked side by side. A green Toyota Avensis and a midnight blue Vauxhall Corsa were parked opposite.

A lithe black woman with short hair came to the door and admitted them, asking to them sign into the visitor's book as they wiped their feet.

"Saw you on the CCTV," she said without being asked. "I assume you're here for Connor? Just follow the corridor round, they're in the dining room."

She walked them a couple of steps and pointed to her right then headed off in the opposite direction and into a door marked 'Office'.

It had been a while since Louis had been here. The place had clearly been given a lick of paint since last time, but there was still something quite cold about the light-yellow walls. Louis spotted a couple of large, black trolley-suitcases by the foot of the stairs along with what looked to be Connor's school bag; he was glad to see that the indignity of bin-liners was apparently a thing of the past. The corridor opened up into a larger room with a high ceiling. A big rectangular dining table with twelve chairs around it filled most of the space. Connor was sat with his back to the two large windows with Aliyah to his right and Elliott to his left. Some music was blaring from his mobile phone as he lectured the two adults about something Louis couldn't quite catch. Louis grinned to himself. Connor looked like he was holding court.

"Issa sound a da police!" Connor exclaimed at the top of his voice, beaming. He was wearing the same red hoody from the night Louis had first met him. His curly hair looked fuller and he seemed to have a healthier glow about him, but Louis could still see the heavy circles beneath his eyes.

Connor stood, pushing past Aliyah's seat, causing her to jolt forward and almost spill her coffee. He came and stood in front of Louis, looking him up and down. Elliott also got to his feet and came to over to Louis and Luke. He proffered his hand to Louis first and they shook. It was a firm handshake, consistent with Elliott's lean but muscular build. His green eyes seemed to shine as he flashed a smile at Louis. "Nice to meet you in the flesh, PC

Mortimer."

He turned to Luke and shook hands.

"Come get in on the action, Big Al," Connor called over to Aliyah, who smiled good-naturedly and rolled her eyes. Connor then turned to Louis. "Beverages, gents?"

"Two coffees, please," Luke piped up, never one to turn down the offer of a hot drink. "Milk and two."

Connor whipped his hand in the air, making a snapping sound with his fingers, then turned and swaggered off merrily through the swinging door behind him to what Louis assumed was the kitchen.

Elliott sat back down at the table with Aliyah. Louis and Luke joined them.

"He seems full of it," remarked Luke, glancing over towards the kitchen suspiciously. "He's not going to spit in our coffee, is he?"

Elliott chuckled, creases appearing at the corners of his eyes.

"He's just buzzing because he got to ride in Elliott's Audi," said Aliyah. "Apparently, my car has zero street-cred. I know he's showing off right now. It's just because he's anxious."

"How long have you been his social worker?" Louis asked.

"Four years and ten placements," replied Aliyah with a weary smile. "He was allocated to me when I was a newly-qualified social worker. They change the social worker when the final court decision is made. The thinking is that a child probably won't want to keep engaging with the social worker that was responsible for removing them from their birth family."

Louis nodded thoughtfully as Aliyah continued.

"He's a pain in the arse but you can't help but love him. Although puberty was a rocky road. He went through that phase of dousing himself in Lynx Africa."

"It's a rite of passage," Luke replied, puffing his chest out with faux pride.

"Makes me gip just thinking about it," laughed Aliyah. "Right, when he comes back, Elliott and I will make ourselves scarce so you can speak to him about last night. We've got to go over his placement and education plans with the staff anyway."

Louis nodded in agreement. He decided that he liked Aliyah. She was intelligent and glamourous but clearly dedicated to her profession. His watch told him it was nearly seven o'clock, way past home time for most social workers he knew.

Connor returned with two steaming mugs of coffee and plonked them down unceremoniously in front of Louis and Luke. "Two coffees."

On cue, Aliyah and Elliott made their excuses and left the dining room. When they had gone, Connor raised his hand to the side of his mouth and spoke in a conspiratorial whisper. "Let me guess, they've told you to ask me about last night?"

"Correct," replied Louis, taking the direct approach. "Where did you go?"

Connor folded his arms in front of him then dropped his head to the table with an exasperated sigh. "Like I keep telling everyone, I don't know. Just, ya know, moving."

"There's a lot of ground to move round. Give me a rough idea."

"Around the city centre mainly," murmured Connor, peeping over his forearms to meet Louis' gaze.

"With anyone?"

"Nope." Connor's face disappeared down behind his arms again.

"Not Wilko?" ventured Louis.

Connor sat up and studied Louis for a few seconds before replying. "I looked for him, but I didn't find him."

"So, you just wandered around all night by yourself?"

"Basically. Why not?" Connor seemed to think about something for a moment before adding, "The city's different at night."

"Has anyone hurt you?" asked Louis, tapping his own neck as prompt to Connor.

He got it and pulled at the collar of his hood, exposing the purplish bruising. "Nah, that was just an accident."

"An accident?"

"Yeah. I climbed a tree."

Louis heard Luke make a muffled noise, as if trying not to cough whilst he had a mouthful of coffee. Evidently, he hadn't been expecting that response either.

"For survival, knobheads," Connor said, rolling his eyes as if it was the most obvious thing in the world. "I went looking for Wilko and some of the other lads in the graveyard next to the hospital. Lots of them go there to drink. When it gets really cold, they can usually find somewhere warm to squat in the grounds."

"So, you slept rough at the hospital?"

"No, I told you, I climbed a tree," repeated Connor. "You think I want to have a cuddle in some scabby bastard's sleeping bag that's probably gonna piss on me in his sleep?"

"Well, when you put it like that...." said Luke, amused.

"I just legged it up a tree and chilled there until the morning. Easy enough to stay out of the way and keep an eye out for people."

Louis marvelled at this prickly, savvy youth. What he was doing was incredibly foolish and risky, but his logic couldn't be faulted.

Connor folded his arms. "Anyway, I keep telling you lot. I wasn't doing anything. I wasn't with anyone. I just needed some space to think and I couldn't be arsed hanging round Becky's. She couldn't wait to get shot of me. We done?"

"I guess so," replied Louis. Connor was already on his feet and padding out of the dining room before Louis had even finished his sentence. A moment later, he heard a door slam upstairs.

Louis and Luke got up and headed back in the direction of the staff office, where they were met by Aliyah and Elliott. Louis summarised what they'd learnt in a low voice. The tale about the tree received bemused grins all round.

With nothing further left to do, they signed out of the visitors' book and the residential worker let them out of the front door. Aliyah was the first to split off, hurrying to her car to get out of the rain. Luke walked in front of Louis and Elliott.

As he fumbled in his jacket for his keys, several documents slipped from the brown paper wallet Elliott was carrying. He cursed and joined Louis in kneeling down to pick them up. Most of them were maths and English worksheets but there was also a glossy pamphlet among them about Special Guardianship. Louis picked up the pamphlet and handed it back to Elliott, who looked a little bashful.

"Just something Aliyah brought me," he said. "Connor's a good kid. Maybe I can do a bit more to help him than teaching him how to add up."

Louis blinked, not sure what to say. Special Guardianship was tantamount to adoption. He recalled his second foster carer had been granted Special Guardianship of a little girl with Down's Syndrome, who had been in her care for since birth. There was no prospect of her returning to her birth mother, but her health needs were too complex for her to stand a chance at being adopted. The Special Guardianship meant that she would no longer be classed as a Looked After Child; no more monthly social worker visits, no more annual health needs assessments, no placement reviews. It was as close to a forever family as some kids could hope for.

"That's great," Louis finally managed. "Good luck."

Elliott smiled, still looking a little awkward, and tucked the pamphlet back in the folder. "Goodnight. Have a safe shift."

Louis watched him get into his car then joined Luke in theirs. Luke was just finishing a point-to-point call via the radio with Sergeant Khan. Apparently, they were being sent to custody to take over the constant watch of a prisoner. Brilliant.

CHAPTER 6

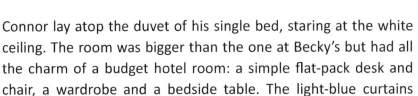

Connor lay atop the duvet of his single bed, staring at the white ceiling. The room was bigger than the one at Becky's but had all the charm of a budget hotel room: a simple flat-pack desk and chair, a wardrobe and a bedside table. The light-blue curtains looked a little threadbare and hung at a strange angle, making Connor wonder if the previous resident had yanked them off the rail at some point.

Jeanette had given him the grand tour. Six bedrooms, only two others of which were currently occupied, on the upper floor along with two bathrooms. The boys had one wing and the only girl had the other. Downstairs was a living room, a chill-out room not dissimilar to the one at Jenkatraz, a laundry room and the staff offices. The kitchen was locked at ten o'clock each night. There were normally three staff members on the day and late shifts, two on the night shift. Jeanette explained that her colleagues had taken the other two residents out to the cinema.

This all seemed fine, Connor thought. Jeanette seemed nice enough. She had offered him the option of being left to his own devices to settle in, or to watch some tv with her for a while. Relieved not to have to submit to enforced family time, Connor had opted to stay in his room. He'd had a shower and changed into some fresh clothes finally, which made him feel better.

Connor wiggled his toes inside his white sport socks. If anyone asked, he kept them on because he always had cold feet. In truth, he never felt fully comfortable unless he was prepared to run. Just before his tenth birthday, he'd remembered hearing the sound of shattering glass. His mum was suddenly in his bedroom, yanking him out from under his covers by the arm. She'd hurried him down the stairs, panting hard. Connor recalled glancing over his shoulder to the kitchen door, where an arm was reaching through the broken glass pane and fumbling to find the yale lock. Emma had pulled him into the living room and helped him climb out of the window into the overgrown front garden before clambering out herself.

As soon as she had hit the ground, she had grabbed Connor's forearm and took off. Connor did his best to keep up, if only to prevent her dragging him down the road. She was wearing her worn black Adidas trainers but he was barefoot, still in his pyjamas. It was July, so the air was still warm and fragrant with the smell of charcoal and spices from the nearby takeaway, despite it being the dead of night. Connor still had no idea who they were running from, but he could see Emma was scared for her life.

They were almost out of the Woodfield estate when Connor realised that he was falling. Emma still had hold of his arm so he fell awkwardly, landing on his side. It took Emma a few seconds to register that Connor was down, meaning that she inadvertently dragged him along the road. Connor cried out as the loose gravel shredded the skin along his ribs and hip. Emma turned and swore under her breath. She wasn't angry with him; he could see that. She was frightened.

Connor tried to stand up but winced in pain, dropping back down again. Blood was pouring from his right foot. He'd stepped on a large chunk of broken glass.

Before they could do anything else, a black car screeched round the corner. Connor shielded his eyes from the searing headlights as it pulled up close to him. He heard the car door swing open. Emma rushed to the driver, who Connor couldn't see from where he lay. All he could hear was Emma babbling before she shrieked in pain. He could see the driver, a bald man with tanned skin in a black t-shirt and a heavy gold chain, had her by her blond hair and was ragging her around like a doll.

Whatever Emma said next must have appeased him because he released her, tossing her in Connor's direction. Connor looked at her tear-streaked face, her eyes now black from her cheap eyeliner smudging. He stayed silent, waiting to follow her lead. His foot was throbbing now. She lifted him up and carried him like a baby towards the back of the car, no mean feat given he was now almost as tall as her and twice as heavy as her emaciated frame. "He's taking us to the hospital, love."

The man drove them quickly to the hospital, warning Emma in a thick accent that Connor couldn't place, not to get blood on his seat. When they pulled up at A&E ten minutes later, he told them unceremoniously to fuck off and disappeared amidst a roar from the car's engine.

That had been the beginning of the end, Connor thought. No one believed Emma that he had accidently cut his foot on a broken glass in the kitchen. At least they didn't accuse her of assaulting him. The social workers started visiting more often after that, almost daily. He remembered them telling her on one visit to see a solicitor because things weren't looking good.

She had really tried. She got him up for school most days. There were times when she was hurting too much to walk him, so he left her and walked the short distance to primary school and lied that she'd brought him. When that happened, she'd always be sure to be at the school gates ready to pick him up, making eye contact with Mrs Andrews, the safeguarding teacher, in a way where she might as well have been sticking two fingers up.

It all went wrong when he opened the door one night without thinking. It was late, maybe eleven o'clock. He had woken up on the sofa to a tapping at the back door. When he'd fallen asleep, Emma had been on the sofa with him watching a film. Maybe she'd nipped to the shop for some cigarettes whilst he was sleeping and forgotten her key.

Connor had gotten up and walked to the back door, which was now boarded up. Still half asleep, he opened it to find strange-looking ginger haired man in a green jacket who introduced himself as Ben and asked where Emma was. Connor caught sight of the council ID badge and knew he must be a social worker. He ran through all the options in his head and eventually let Ben in, telling him that Emma had just nipped to the shop.

Nearly an hour had passed with no sign of Emma. Ben left Connor in the living room and went into the kitchen to make a phone call. Whoever he was speaking to, he was telling them that the police would need to come and PPO Connor, whatever that meant, and an emergency foster placement had to be authorised.

That was his last night in Woodfield Crescent. When the cops arrived, they handed Police Protection Order papers to Ben, who then took Connor in his car to a grand-looking house on the outskirts of the city. His normal social worker came to see him the following day, telling him that Emma was safe but Connor would be staying in foster care until a judge could decide whether he could go back to her.

Connor turned ten years old sat in a family contact room at the Social Services office. Emma had arrived with a twin-pack of cupcakes and a candle. They sat on the floor, under the watchful gaze of the contact supervisor, as Emma lit the candle, placed it in one of the cupcakes and sang to him. They were supposed to go for a pizza as well, but Connor lied and said he wasn't hungry. He could see that Emma was physically in pain. He helped her up onto the sofa and sat next to her, leaning on her bony arm and feeling the prickle of her brittle blond curls against his cheek as he showed her pictures on his phone.

Connor blinked hard, suddenly realising he was crying silent tears. He rolled over into a foetal position and let them fall, never making a sound.

* * * * *

Louis stretched his legs out in front of him and used his heels to roll himself back and forth gently in the officer chair he sat on outside the open cell door. Just beyond the threshold, a huddled shape shivered underneath a heap of pale green blankets on top of a blue mattress. Mattress was perhaps too generous a description for what actually resembled a gym mat, Louis thought. The prisoner had finally calmed down from whatever chemical-induced rage, so Luke had taken the opportunity to fetch some coffees.

Louis was never particularly fond of coming down to the custody block below Weaver's Yard Police Station. At best, there always seemed to be a pervasive fug of stale alcohol, sweaty feet and disinfectant; at worst, the stench of a dirty protest from someone particularly unhappy with the accommodations. Today was fortunately not one of those days, but someone had been banging and screaming in a cell round the corner for the last half an hour.

61

As long as he didn't wake this idiot up again, Louis thought grimly.

Luke reappeared with two plastic coffee cups. Before sitting down in the other chair, he crossed over into the cell, peered at the prisoner to satisfy himself that he was still breathing, then joined Louis.

Louis gratefully accepted the cup but couldn't help pulling a face when he tasted the acrid brew.

"Nothing but the finest for our guests," said Luke with a wry smile. "So then, what's your bet that young Connor doesn't go tonight?"

"A bag of Mini-Eggs," replied Louis. He had quickly become accustomed to Luke's confectionary-related bets at the beginning of his tutorship. There was no malice in it.

Luke sucked air through his gritted teeth. "You must be confident."

"I'm not really." Louis looked down into his cup and swirled the liquid, pondering for a moment. "I think he's trying to find his mum."

"Go on?" There was no joking in Luke's tone this time.

Louis frowned, organising his thoughts to make sure he wasn't talking rubbish. "Well, if she's on the game and hitting the drugs hard, she'll more than likely be moving with the rough sleepers and street drinkers. If she's no-fixed-abode, maybe Connor's hanging around places that he reckons she might turn up at."

Luke nodded thoughtfully. "Makes sense. Let's hope he hasn't been hanging around on Garnett Street though."

"Surely the type of curb crawlers that pass through there aren't looking for kids?" said Louis, suddenly feeling a chill of worry. "Especially a little gobshite like Connor."

They were both distracted by a sound that fell somewhere between a yawn and a moan from their prisoner. The lump of blankets shifted briefly then fell still again.

"Annie ran a job that stemmed from Garnett Street a couple of years ago," Luke said, once he was happy that the prisoner was settled. "Some of the women down there reported that there was an underage girl selling. Only it turned out that the girl was a boy. Wigs, make-up, but all the original parts if you get me? A lot of the pervs that picked her up weren't too bothered about what was going on down there. Some were even into it."

Louis listened closely, feeling a pang of sorrow for the child. Luke's wife was a detective in the Child Protection Unit, meaning that he often regaled Louis with heartbreaking tales.

"So, the kid starts to get a bit bolder," Luke continued. "You know, going out as a boy but wearing girl's clothes, or getting dolled up above the shoulders but wearing stuff that left people in no doubt she was a boy down there. It works for her for a little while because of the novelty value, but eventually it backfires. This punter picks her up, knowing full well what she is, and drives her behind the abattoir to do business."

Louis grimaced, not liking where this was going.

"Before she has chance to go to work on him, he batters her senseless with a piece of copper pipe he'd had up his sleeve. After he's beaten the kid to a bloody pulp, of course he decides this would be the time to rape her. Some poor bastard got the shock of his life when he came to throw stuff in the wheelie bins and found her body stuffed between two of them."

"He killed her?"

"She was barely alive," Luke replied gravely. "It took ages for them to fix her jaw and get her looking half-way human again. Two fractured eye sockets and multiple skull fractures as well as internal injuries. Annie kept going to see her in hospital, checking in on her. The family had disowned her so she had no one. Eventually, she agreed to do a video interview. They got the guy that attacked her, plus a few of the nonces that picked her up and her so-called landlord that was taking a cut of her earnings."

"I remember it now," said Louis. "He pleaded to GBH rather than attempted murder."

"Yeah," Luke shook his head sadly. "Annie lost her shit when she heard. They accepted GBH without intent because they weren't certain they could prove that he intended to do her serious harm."

Louis was incredulous. "He'd battered her with a pipe! What more did they want?"

"Exactly what Annie said. His defence was that he thought he'd picked up a woman, and when it turned out it was a male, he tried to leave and the victim produced the pipe and tried to rob him."

"The victim was a kid, for fuck's sake!" Louis lowered his voice quickly when he spotted the custody sergeant looking over at him from the desk down the corridor.

"I know. But no way CPS wanted to take the chance of explaining all that to a jury. He got the full five years, mind. The kid was ok with it. By that point, she just wanted to try and move on from it all."

Louis sighed heavily and looked down at his feet again. "You could have just said Connor could be at risk from hanging around on Garnett Street."

Luke laughed and shrugged. "We're cops. We like to tell stories."

After he moment, he said, "Maybe Child Protection is something you should think about as your next move. You're practically signed off now, or at least you will be when I finish writing up your final assessments."

Louis turned to look at Luke. He knew the advice was well-meaning but he couldn't help feeling like he'd let Luke down somehow. "Don't you think I can cut it on patrol?"

"Of course you can, mate," Luke replied. He made a sweeping gesture with his arm, causing himself to spin round in his chair. "You can do all this. At the end of the day, it's just using your brain, knowing how to talk to people and being a bit handy when you need to be. You've got all that. But you've also got a talent for working with vulnerable people. Pub fights and street robberies, you can take or leave, but I see you light up when we go to a domestic or a safeguarding job. Look at how you've been with Connor. I see you doing great things, my friend."

Louis almost believed him. "I'll think about it."

"Course you will," said Luke, giving him a gentle shove that made him roll a couple of centimetres. "Bollocks. We had a bit of a moment there. Let me go scrounge us some chocolate from the custody tuck shop. I'm an emotional eater, you know."

"Dickhead," Louis replied with a laugh, watching his mentor swagger off down the corridor. "I'll check the logs and see if I owe you any Mini Eggs."

* * * * *

Bryan Hillesley smiled when he saw a chat window pop up on his screen from blueeyedboi14.

"WUU2?" followed by an angel emoji. What you up to?

"Waiting for you to show up," Bryan typed, lying shamelessly. He clicked off a couple of photos he'd been perusing and brought up blueeyedboi14's instead. Annoyingly, the only real photos he would send were of his face. Everything else was computer-generated. Bryan could live with it though. Not everyone could be expected to have same knowledge and resources that allowed Bryan to indulge his guilty pleasures with minimal fear of detection. Plus, those blue eyes and full lips were irresistible. He typed another message. "Nice day at school?"

"Yh."

"Not very talkative tonight, babe?"

It was a moment before the reply came. "Just worried if I tell u something u'll be mad."

Bryan bit his thumb gently then typed, "Tell me."

"What would you do if......."

Bryan drummed his fingers impatiently waiting for the next message. "If what?"

"If I said there was someone else I liked?"

Bryan clenched his jaw. "Ur teacher?"

"Sum1 else."

Bryan sat back in his chair for a moment, pushing the tip of his tongue back and forth against the inside of his right cheek. He stared intently at blueeyedboi14's photo. A lump in his throat made him swallow hard. Then he sat forward again and began to type.

"Grab you by your hair and drag you around the living room......throw you on the sofa and punch ur face.......choke you with one hand….."

Bryan kept typing, his words becoming more obscene. As quickly as he sent more messages, blueeyedboi14 started sending back images. Bruises on his cheeks and around his eyes. His pale torso, also bruised. A hand around his throat, choking the life out of him – a different image this time to the one from the other night. Bryan didn't care that they were computer generated, they were enough.

After a few more minutes in that vein, there was no further need to continue.

"I'm sorry. I shouldn't have made you mad."

"Not mad anymore," Bryan typed, wiping his brow with the back of his hand. "Just want you to myself."

"Cd be arranged."

"Are you a cop?"

No sooner had he typed the question, an image popped up that left Bryan in no doubt that blueeyedboi14 was the genuine article. Bryan stared closely at the image for another moment to satisfy himself that it wasn't another computer generation, then started typing again.

CHAPTER 7

Connor didn't remember falling asleep. As he started to become more aware of his surroundings, he felt something close to his face. He forced his eyes open. A pair of brown eyes blinked back at him. He jumped up with a start, launching himself back-first into the wall next to his bed.

The girl who had been knelt down by his bed jumped to her feet, shrieking in fright herself.

"The fuck you doing?" Connor growled, not quite awake enough to form full sentences.

"Well, that's rude!" his visitor exclaimed, folding her arms and leaning back.

Connor rubbed his eyes and studied her properly. A pale, waif-like kid with long brown hair piled up into a messy bun atop her head, she wore a black sparkly top and spray-on blue jeans. She was tall even without the heeled boots she was wearing.

"I'm Ariana," she announced. As if on cue, the bedroom door opened and a short, rough-looking boy wearing a black Nike tracksuit shuffled in. "This is Jimmy."

Connor guessed they were both around his age. He peered over Ariana's shoulder, watching carefully as Jimmy wandered around the room to check out Connor's belongings.

"Staff took us out to the movies," Ariana said, once more answering an unasked question. She reached her hand out to Connor. "M&Ms?"

Connor extended his hand cautiously and accepted a handful of her sweets. He glanced across at the bedside table and scooped up his mobile phone before Jimmy got his hands on it. There was a text message from an unknown number. He thrust the phone into his pocket.

"Night staff come on at ten," said Ariana She hopped onto the bed and sat next to him with her back to the wall. "They take our phones off us at ten-thirty. If you're chatting to anyone you better tell them in case they wonder why you suddenly go quiet."

Connor nodded in acknowledgement. Jimmy had finished his inspection of the room and joined them on the bed, sitting on Connor's other side.

"Got any weed?" he asked. He spoke with a bit of a drawl, which Connor figured was more to do with a speech impediment than being stoned.

"Jimmy, you div!" cried Ariana, pointing at Connor's inhaler on the bedside table. "He's got asthma, he can't smoke!"

"I don't have any weed," Connor replied, already weary of this bizarre double-act. "No booze either."

"No worries," said Ariana, patting Connor's thigh. "So, do you like girls or boys?"

"Mind your own fucking business!" growled Connor, jumping off the bed to his feet.

Ariana and Jimmy creased up laughing on the bed. Fighting for breath, Ariana giggled, "Chill, mush! It's just a question. I like boys. Jimmy likes boys and girls."

"Good for you," he snorted.

The door opened again and Jeanette popped her head around. "Getting acquainted, I see. Come on, you two, you should know better. Let Connor get settled in."

The two teenagers huffed and slid off the bed, making for the door. Connor jumped as he felt one of them give his bottom a playful squeeze.

"Fucking weirdos," he muttered under his breath.

After they had left, Jeanette said, "We've got a house rule that everyone stays out of each other's rooms. These two are alright, to be fair, but unfortunately things have been known to go missing. Make sure to keep your door locked when you're not in."

Connor nodded, sticking his hands into his pockets.

Jeanette smiled warmly and gave his arm a gentle squeeze. "You'll be ok here, love. The kitchen's getting locked in ten minutes but I'll make you a hot chocolate if you want?"

"That'd be nice, ta."

Connor waited for the door to close then pulled his phone out to read his new message. His eyes widened when he saw the text. He quickly opened the door and peered out into the hallway. No one there. He sauntered down the hall, following the sound of pop music to one of the doors in the girls' wing. He tapped on the door urgently, not wanting to be too loud in case Jeanette came back.

The door was flung open and Ariana beamed at him. "Hi!"

Connor shushed her and held a finger to his lips, then whispered, "How do I get out of here?"

"Either you persuade your social worker or you turn sixteen," replied Ariana, fluttering her ridiculous false eyelashes at him.

"I mean how do I get to town, idiot!" hissed Connor.

"Aw, you've got no chance now, chicken," replied Ariana, her eyes lighting up. "The kitchen fire escape's the best way but they're locking the kitchen up now. Otherwise, the only way to do it is setting the fire alarm off because it makes all the outside doors unlock. Don't do that though, cos they'll charge you money. Why do you want to go to town?"

"To meet someone," he replied, pausing to think.

"Ooo, who? Have you got a girlfriend?" Ariana didn't wait for the answer. "You're better off staying out all day then not coming home. That way, they can't call the police to get after you or chase the bus. They do that, you know. Once, me and Jimmy jumped on the night bus and the staff followed it in their car and rung the bus company to make them stop so they could get us."

Connor took that information on board, weighing up his options. He heard Jeanette's voice in the hallway downstairs calling to another staff member. He thanked Ariana hurriedly and darted back towards his room.

"It was Jimmy that pinched your bum, by the way!" she called out in a faux whisper after him.

Connor got to his doorway just before Jeanette came up the stairs with his drink. She said goodnight and reminded him that he needed to be in bed asleep by eleven. Connor thanked her and went back into his room. He sat on the edge of his bed and pulled his phone back out. Finally, the message he'd been waiting for.

"U ok CJ?"

CJ. Connor James. He didn't recognise the number but it had to be her. Only Emma called him CJ. He pressed the screen to dial the number. An automated voice immediately told him that the phone's owner couldn't take calls right now and that there was no voicemail option.

Frustration gave way as a new message popped up. "Can't speak now, son. U ok?"

Connor blinked back tears. No, he fucking wasn't ok. "Yh. Where ru?"

"Staying with friend nr Garnett St. Im safe tho, ru?"

Connor didn't want to worry her. "Yh."

Three messages came back in quick succession.

"Will cu soon CJ, missed u so much," followed by a row of heart emojis.

Finally, "Don't tell ne1 I msg u or give this number k."

"K. Send me a pic."

Connor waited, grasping the phone tight. If only he could see a picture of her and know she was ok. After a few minutes, nothing had arrived. Downstairs, he heard the front door buzz and the sound of new voices. Night staff, he guessed. Remembering what Ariana had said, he turned his phone off and slid it under his pillow. He wasn't about to hand his phone over unless they asked for it, but if they did, they wouldn't be able to see any new messages on his front screen. Connor slid under the covers and turned off his light. Garnett Street. He was finally going to see Emma.

* * * * *

The custody block had eventually calmed down around five in the morning, like a sort of witching hour had befallen the place. The buzz picked back up an hour later though as detention officers began rousing prisoners, offering breakfast and showers for those due to be collected for transport to court.

Louis was scrolling through the morning news on his handheld terminal, occasionally checking through the incident logs and hoping not to see Connor's name. Luke was sat in his chair with his eyes closed and arms folded, insisting that he was just resting his eyes. They were both exhausted. At half-past three, just before their shift was due to end, a broadcast went across the airwaves advising all half-night units were to remain on duty until further notice. It wasn't uncommon, particularly when demand was high throughout the city.

Luke jerked as his radio suddenly chirped, signalling someone was point-to-pointing him. He popped his earpiece back in and answered. Whoever it was, they were delivering good news.

"Sarge is sending a couple of early-turn down to relieve us," Luke said. "At least we'll be off on time."

Louis stood up and stretched, his lower back numb from being sat so long. "I'm going to hit the gym before I go. You coming?"

Luke shook his head. "Annie's on earlies so we'll have to do a car-park handover. Thank god for Breakfast Club."

Louis remembered being amazed in his early days how many police officers did that. He'd sit in his car in the staff car park waiting for his shift to start, watching officers coming off duty, being greeted with a brief hug and kiss at the family car, then waving goodbye as their partners walked off into the station to begin their shift. Luke had introduced him to Annie and their kids on one such handover; Evie, the slender blonde seven-year-old, favoured Annie whilst five-year old Polly, with her dark hair and mischievous face, was Luke's double. They'd shrieked with delight and clung to Luke's long legs, thrilled to see him. Louis remembered smiling awkwardly. He envied those family bonds shamelessly but didn't begrudge them for a second.

Within twenty minutes, two officers arrived and took a handover from them. They locked their radios and PAVA away then headed to the changing rooms. Luke hung up his tac-vest and body armour in his locker, replacing them with a nondescript grey hoody. It was by no means a foolproof disguise as anyone who looked down at Luke's black cargo trousers and immaculate leather boots would easily guess his occupation. Meanwhile, Louis changed into a pair of black shorts and a blue t-shirt.

"If you're not too knackered afterwards, nip up and see Annie in the Child Protection office," said Luke. "She'll introduce you to the DI. Doesn't hurt to make your interest known."

Louis looked up from tying his black Nike running shoes with a wry grin. "I don't know if I'm interested yet."

"You will be," said Luke, nodding and smiling like a man who couldn't have been more certain. He then slapped Louis a high-five and went on his way.

Louis did some dynamic stretches, keen to get going before his motivation deserted him. Thirty minutes of cardio and he would be homeward-bound. When he was ready, he walked to the back of the locker room and entered the gym via a connecting door. It was a large space with a decent assortment of free weights, machines and cardio equipment.

As Louis crossed the room to the treadmills, he spotted Damien in the free weights area; otherwise, the gym was empty. Louis grimaced. At least when he was working out with Luke, they kept up a good banter whilst pushing each other. He didn't expect Damien would be particularly chatty but at least his presence would prevent Louis from quitting early.

He was right. Damien finished his set of overhead presses and turned round, hands on hips, to catch his breath. When he saw Louis, he offered little more than a nod to acknowledge him. Louis nodded back nonchalantly, inserting his Airpods and dropping his water bottle into the holder on the treadmill. To the electronic beats of a trance playlist, Louis quickly built up his pace until he reached a steady 12kmph.

As he relaxed into the run, Louis let his mind drift to other things. He felt reassured that Connor hadn't been reported missing overnight. Maybe Aliyah was right that the care home environment would work better for him. Louis supposed it would be hard on some level for a kid like Connor, so fiercely devoted to his mum, to engage with a foster family for fear of appearing disloyal. That made him think of Elliott. Sure, he and Connor seemed to have a good relationship but would that change if Elliott tried to become Connor's carer? Louis hoped not. If Elliott could just navigate Connor through his adolescence safely, there might be hope.

Louis didn't doubt for a moment that Elliott could see Connor through. He was smart and confident, absolutely the type of role model Connor could look up to. Handsome as hell too. Louis blushed as soon as the thought popped into his mind.

In pushing Elliott out of his mind, Louis found himself focussing on Damien, who had resumed overhead presses with a massive barbell. His black shorts and grey Metallica vest did little to soften Damien's appearance. Louis couldn't help but appreciate the brooding man-mountain, whose tattooed arms rippled as if they were alive of their own accord. As he lowered the barbell to the floor, the tension in his legs made them look as if they had been carved from granite. When he stood up and wiped the sweat from his forehead, he turned slightly and looked over in Louis' direction. His lean, stubbly face was just as chiselled as the rest of his body, like a model from an aftershave ad. Louis prayed his own expression looked vacant, or at least focussed on his run.

Louis' thoughts returned to Connor's situation. No one at the planning meeting had mentioned Connor's father. Would he object to someone like Elliott taking Connor on? Louis assumed he wasn't on the scene or, at least, wasn't someone good for Connor to be around. Then again, Louis recalled the professionals working with him as a child being completely dismissive of his dad. He was around, somewhere, but there never seemed to be any particular interest in encouraging him to attend meetings or family contact. All the focus was on his mum. Louis' hopes and dreams of returning to something like a normal life lived or died with her ability to prove to the social workers that she was ok.

Louis cranked up the speed as unwelcome memories of his dad flooded into his consciousness. Loud, sometimes violent, constantly slurring from the rum he drank. The rows he would have with Louis' mum. Plates smashing, screaming, normally followed the arrival of the police. Louis wished he could say it was all bad. Dealing in absolutes was always easier. But he also remembered his dad's warm, honey-like voice with the lilt of a French accent, singing songs and telling him stories about

Mauritius. His black, curly hair and deep-brown skin. The blend of those exotic genes with his mum's white European ones had given Louis an attractive, toned-down version of his dad's looks. And the smell of delicious, spicy food when his dad would cook. Louis clenched his fists and ran harder, feeling his quads burning.

He barely registered Damien standing in front of him, looking at the speed on the treadmill screen with an impressed expression. Louis met his dark-blue eyes and felt a chill as they seemed to pierce him. Damien gave Louis a thumbs-up accompanied by a quizzical cocking of one eyebrow. OK? he mouthed. Louis returned the thumbs up, catching sight of his frantic reflection in the mirrors on the opposite wall.

Damien stepped onto the neighbouring treadmill and started a brisk jog. Louis dialled down the speed on his own machine, feeling ready to cool down now. He kept glancing sideways at Damien, who was picking up his own pace. The man really was a wall of solid muscle. Louis wondered whether he should speak but decided against it. Damien was breathing harder now. He probably wouldn't welcome idle chit-chat, Louis convinced himself. As the treadmill slowed to a brisk walk, Louis used the remaining time to try and pick out the images form the tattoo sleeve on Damien's right arm: skulls, ravens, roses...

"I can tell you the guy that did it, if you want?"

Shit! Louis paused his music and tried to cover himself by taking a swig from his water before replying, "Yeah, sure. Just...looks good on you, mate. Not sure I could carry it off though."

"Check out his flash on Facebook if you've got it," replied Damien, having no difficulty with holding a conversation despite his speed creeping up to 12kmph now. "Duke of the Black Crown. He's in Glasgow but it's worth the journey"

"Cool, cool," said Louis, bringing his treadmill to a halt. "Well, that's me done."

"See you tonight, pal," Damien replied. Then his gaze was straight ahead again, his focus seemingly back on his workout.

Louis fought the urge to scurry off into the nearest dark corner and die of embarrassment. He was wracked with the same shameful feelings he used to have as a teenager looking at other lads in the changing room, realising the uncomfortable truth that he was wired a little differently. He dug his index fingernail into his thumb, grounding himself in the present moment and reassuring himself that Damien would have thought nothing of it. It worked to a degree. Louis gathered his things up from the locker room and headed for the showers.

CHAPTER 8

Louis looked round the briefing room. The half-nights team looked sparser than usual thanks to the various winter bugs that were doing the rounds. Louis sat with Sharlene to his right. Damien sat beside her and Luke was at the end. Sergeant Khan, a wiry man in his late forties, stood in front of them, running through various briefing items on the big LCD screen behind him. Once he had finished, he began assigning duties.

"Sharlene, appointments. Louis, our resident missing-person whisperer, MISPER car. Luke, Damien, get tasered up please, gents. You can go out as a double-crewed unit."

"Yes!" exclaimed Luke, holding up his fist for Damien to bump it. Louis grinned, knowing he was deliberately winding Damien up. Eventually, Damien touched his fist to Luke's with all the enthusiasm of someone waiting to have a tooth removed.

Luke ruffled Damien's hair excitedly. "My man!"

Louis looked on as Damien tried to tidy himself up. Whatever aftershave he was wearing, it was crisp and fresh. The five o'clock shadow he had been sporting this morning had since gone.

"Save the bromance for the car, lads," Sergeant Khan said wearily.

"Full nights are on at ten but they're limited on numbers as well, so we might as well prepare ourselves for being kept on."

Sharlene kissed her teeth loudly then cursed under her breath.

"Come on, Sharl, think of the overtime!" said Luke, rubbing his fingertips together and raising his eyebrows suggestively.

"I'd rather think about getting into my nice warm bed with my man," she grumbled, pulling out her phone to send a text message.

"Well, seeing as it's the last night and we're gonna be kept on, what about a carvery breakfast in the morning?"

"Cos we don't see enough of you as it is?" murmured Damien, smiling wryly as he typed out a message on his own phone.

"You lot absolutely fucking love it!" replied Luke. "I'll put it in the group chat and see who bites. Besides, we've got something to celebrate."

Louis joined everyone else in looking at Luke in anticipation.

Satisfied he had everyone's attention, he continued. "My young padawan is officially signed off."

Sharlene shrieked and pulled Louis to her, kissing his forehead loudly. "Yes, man! Remember now, that's a cream cake fine."

Louis nodded gravely, making note to buy a set of cream buns for the team on the next shift as per tradition.

"Well done, Louis," said Sergeant Khan, shaking his hand. "Have this list of MISPER enquiries in lieu of a gift. Come on then, let's crack on."

As they shuffled out of the briefing room, Louis felt a large hand land heavily on his right shoulder.

"Nice one, mate," Damien said with the slightest smile. Before Louis could say anything, Luke barged into Damien, encircling his arms around his waist and driving him onwards in a semi-serious rugby tackle towards the Taser storeroom.

"Dickheads," tutted Sharlene, steering Louis towards the report room. "Come on, darling, we'll brew up."

* * * * *

"Ahhh!"

Connor's head jerked up. "What?"

Ariana thrust her phone at his face. The picture on it showed a teenage boy that looked like he'd applied every filter available. "He's added me on SnapChat!"

"Fuck's sake, man," grumbled Connor, looking around the McDonalds they were currently sat in and hoping nobody had noticed Ariana's high-pitched squeak. Fortunately, the place was starting to fill with revellers in various stages of inebriation. He looked at his own phone. The clock read nine-thirty. Still early.

He'd decided to follow Ariana's advice to give himself the best chance of slipping away from the children's home without being dragged back too soon. Ariana and Jimmy had tagged along, much to his annoyance; then again, it probably looked more natural for them to be moving in a group rather than just Connor by himself.

He'd messaged Emma a few more times during the day but nothing came back. He'd barely resisted the urge to try ringing her, remembering that she might not be safe to talk. He touched his thumb to the keypad to unlock his phone, bringing up the Map App. Garnett Street was only a ten-minute walk away. He figured there would be no point heading over there too early because Emma was more of a night-owl.

It had inevitably meant spending the day with Ariana and Jimmy. Connor begrudgingly admitted that it had been fun. Ariana was incapable of having a quiet thought, a quality that made her strangely disarming. Jimmy was more sober but his dry, blunt observations made him the perfect foil for Ariana. There was something quite nice about hanging out with other kids with a similar background.

Ariana, he learned, had been removed from her mother before the age of one. Her mum had already had two children taken from her. The judge had been swayed by an enthusiastic Guardian ad Litem, a social worker independent from the local authority, to allow a residential assessment period. Ariana and her mother moved in with a foster carer, whose job was to support and assess her parenting capacity. Ariana's mother had walked out after three weeks, disappearing until shortly before the final court hearing.

Adoption was supposed to be the happily-ever-after ending. Ariana had been adopted by an affluent family from the suburbs. No one could have known that her adoptive father had gone through with it as a way to distract her adoptive mother from the affair he was having with his business partner. It all came out when Ariana was nine, sending her mother into turmoil. The final straw was finding Ariana and her adoptive cousin of a similar age with their underwear down in Ariana's bedroom, curiously observing the difference in their bodies. Her mother had screamed at Ariana, slapped her twice across the face and driven her to the nearest social services office with a bin bag of clothes. Despite every effort over the following months, Ariana's mother refused to have her back.

Jimmy was a different story. Chronically neglected from birth, he had heard the term 'failure to thrive' used to describe him for as long as he could remember. Somehow, the local authority had stayed optimistic about his mother. She tried hard, everyone used to say about her.

No one had been particularly bothered when six-year-old Jimmy started telling them that he hated doing the washing up. At least she's giving him a clean plate to eat off, his class teacher had remarked in a review meeting, much to everyone's amusement. Jimmy persisted with his complaint, right until the last day of term before the summer holidays. He waited until the other kids had left the classroom, charging out towards six weeks of freedom, then repeated his objection to his learning mentor.

"Oh, give it a rest, lad!" she'd said brusquely as she tidied the paint pots next to the sink, not bothering to make eye contact. "I hate doing the washing up too, but sometimes we just have to shut up and get on with things."

Jimmy had nodded sullenly and skulked out of the classroom. Three weeks later, he was admitted to hospital with serious rectal bleeding. A social worker had sat with him at the bedside flanked by a child protection detective. When he told her he had gotten hurt whilst washing up, she asked him what washing up was. Jimmy spoke quietly, fearful that he would receive a slap for saying it out loud. Washing up in his house involved his mum's boyfriend putting his penis in Jimmy's bottom. He never went back home.

Ariana and Jimmy told their stories matter-of-factly, barely any emotion on their faces. Connor understood it. Every professional they met, whether at school, at home or when they went to the doctor for a cough wanted to know. After a while, it was just a meaningless stream of words.

"They're going to be ringing us soon," Ariana said with a weary sigh.

"Fuck 'em," Connor murmured. As if on cue, his phone flashed with an incoming call. He answered it without speaking. It was a staff member from Robin Hill. He hung up. "Come on, let's go."

He marched towards the door, zipping up his black hooded jacket. The benefit of time had been the chance to plan properly. He had put layers of warm clothes on and stuffed his pockets with food. He'd find his mum tonight no matter what. Ariana and Jimmy followed him, Ariana pausing long enough to gather up the rest of her chips to bring with her.

As they moved through the city to the northern edge, the drunken, fashionably-clad revellers made way for the more hard-bitten elements. Grizzled men and leathery women standing outside pubs smoking stared at them curiously as they walked past.

Occasionally, Ariana would move in closer and say hi. Connor carried on marching towards his destination, leaving Jimmy to pull Ariana by the arm so she would continue following them.

They eventually reached a mini-roundabout with three exits ahead. Connor stopped and checked his phone. Garnett Street was the first exit on the right. He turned and looked each way, preparing to cross.

"Why you going down there?" Jimmy asked, concern in his voice.

"To meet my mum," said Connor impatiently.

Jimmy took a step back. "It's bad down there, man. You shouldn't go."

"It's just another street where people live," snapped Connor, growing more exasperated.

Ariana linked her arm with Jimmy's. "He's right, babes. Jimmy's been down there before. A lot. The people around there are bad."

"What the fuck are you on about?"

"Duh!" Ariana slapped her forehead. "It's where you go to sell your arse."

Jimmy nodded sombrely. "Don't go, Connor. They won't care that you're a kid."

"You two are fucking tapped!" Connor started crossing the road towards Garnett Street. When he reached half way, he looked over his shoulder. Jimmy and Ariana were still standing there. "Don't tell anyone where I am, dickheads!"

Connor was relieved when he saw them turn and begin to walk back to town. He felt bad for yelling at them. They were only trying to help in their weird way, but it was better that they weren't with him when he found Emma. There was a lot of catching up to do and the last thing he needed was Ariana asking her fucking stupid questions and Jimmy nicking Emma's stuff. He pulled up his hood and started walking down Garnett Street, his eyes scanning the gloom for any sign of Emma.

* * * * *

"X-ray three-one."

Louis took his right hand off the steering wheel of the police car and pushed the talk button on his radio. "Three-one"

"Three-one, can you expedite to Robin Hill Children's Home. Report of a fourteen-year-old child in care missing from home."

Louis gritted his teeth. Connor.

Before he could reply, Sharlene's voice came over. "X-ray three-three, I've come free from my last appointment. I'll attend the home and get take the missing report. Let three-one start making enquiries in the city."

The operator was happy with that. "Three-three, that's received."

Louis was grateful for the assistance. He was at least half an hour away from Robin Hill and didn't yet have his emergency response permit. No blue-lighting for now.

Luke's voice came through next. "Tango three-four, we'll take a drive through the city and see if we can spot him."

The 'tango' element of the callsign denoted that Luke and Damien were carrying tasers. Louis acknowledged the transmission and pulled his car over to read the incident log properly on his handheld terminal. Connor had been out all day with two other residents from the home. When the children's home staff had called them at nine-thirty to find out where they were and received no response, they reported all three children missing. They had subsequently made contact with the girl, who said they were on the bus heading home. She had hung up without confirming whether or not Connor was with them. If Luke had been with him, Louis would have gladly bet a bag of Mini-Eggs that Connor wasn't on that bus.

* * * * *

Connor dug his hands deeper into his pockets and looked around. The wind had picked up and was cutting through the layers he had on, making his teeth chatter. He was midway down Garnett Street at this point. There were a couple of sets of maisonette flats on one side and a court of small terraced council houses on the other. The street was quiet, save for the odd car that cruised past. A strange stench hit his nostrils hard. He looked out into the distance and saw a plume of smoke rising from a tall chimney then remembered something Elliott had told him about the abattoir.

Connor shivered again. For just a second, he was tempted to call Elliott, who had given him his number a long time ago if he was ever in a crisis. He quickly dismissed the idea. Elliott would more than likely come and scoop him up.

He dug his phone out of his pocket and rang Emma's number. The same electronic message told him that she wasn't available. He let out a frustrated roar and kicked the junction box next to him. Then, like some divine answer to his prayers, she appeared. Emma was walking towards him, blond curls bouncing as she moved. She was wearing skin-tight black jeans and a red halter-top

"Mam!" Connor ran forward. He only got a few feet before skidding to a halt. The woman looked old enough to be his grandmother, not that he knew his grandmother.

"Sorry, darling," she drawled, pulling on a cigarette. "You're not one of mine."

"Emma McAllen," Connor gasped, trying to pull himself together. "Is she here?"

"I 'ant seen her for a fair while, darling," she replied. "She does come round here though, usually a bit later on."

Connor's heart sank as he understood what the woman was telling him. "Does she live round here?"

The woman had turned away from him and stepped to the edge of the pavement, eying up a blue Audi that slowed down as it approached her. When it had moved out of sight, she replied, "No-one really lives round here, love. She might be in one of the flats though. Are you her kid?"

Connor nodded.

The woman reached into her handbag and passed him a strip of chewing gum. "You probably won't listen to me, but just fuck off out of here, darling. The people that hang around here aren't good."

"I need to find her!" Connor cried out, exposing more emotion than he intended to with this stranger.

"Look, sweetheart, if she's on here, she won't want you to see her," the woman said matter-of-factly. "I'm going to be around for a bit, ok, so come and find me if you need help. Better if you just go home, though."

Before Connor could ask her anything else, the same blue Audi cruised back up towards them. The woman sauntered over to the driver's window and greeted him like a dear old friend before getting into the passenger seat. Connor watched the car drive off then turned his gaze towards the flats.

CHAPTER 9

A few hours had passed with no result. Luke and Damien had been diverted to an emergency call, so Louis had taken over searching the city for Connor in vain. He had even rattled Wilko the street-drinker's cage when he'd spotted him, but Wilko swore blind that he hadn't seen Connor.

He pulled the car over again to check the log and update it with his own enquiries. Louis slapped the steering wheel in frustration. His radio chirped, signalling a point-to-point call. He answered brusquely.

Sharlene's voice came through. "He's on Garnett Street."

Louis started the car and headed in that direction. "Says who?"

"The kids he was with have just landed back at the home. They left him there because they didn't want to go. He said something about looking for his mum. Standby and I'll blue-light over."

Louis wasn't about to sit waiting for Sharlene. He carried on driving, kicking himself mentally for not thinking about Garnett Street sooner. How did Connor even know to go there?

The operator's voice came over. "Three-three, can I divert you to back up a single-crewed nights unit going to an emergency domestic."

"Yes, yes," Sharlene replied, frustration in her voice.

Louis kept going, pushing the car to go as fast as possible without committing a speeding offence. After what felt like an eternity, he pulled into Garnett Street. There was no movement, just mist and the dull glow of streetlights. He had no choice but to crawl along slowly, head shifting from side to side in the hope of spotting Connor.

As he moved further along the street, he saw a woman with peroxide-blonde curls leaning against a junction box. He pulled the police car alongside her and lowered the passenger window.

She leaned in and smiled. "Business, darling?"

"No, thanks," Louis replied civilly. Nor did he have any interest in making an issue of the fact that she'd just offered sex to an on-duty police officer. "I'm looking for a missing kid."

The soft, sweet voice suddenly became altogether rougher. "Blond curly hair? He's been up and down here all night. He's knocking on doors looking for his mum."

Louis gritted his teeth. "When did you last see him?"

"'Bout five minutes ago, darling," she replied. "Poor lad, he's frantic trying to find Emma."

Louis reached into his patrol bag on the back seat and drew out a chocolate bar and a can of Red Bull. He offered it to the woman. "Mind how you go, yeah?"

She nodded and smiled, taking the items from him then setting off down the road.

Luke set the car in motion again and cruised up Garnett Street. When he reached the end, he turned round and retraced his route. He spotted Connor walking out of the courtyard leading to the adjacent flats. Instinct took over and he revved the car to reach Connor quickly. He hit the curb with a bump that rocked him hard.

Connor snapped his head round for a second then took off running.

Louis leapt from the car and ran after him. His legs still burned from his workout that morning but the adrenaline allowed him to power through. He was on Connor within seconds, grabbing hold of his shoulder and upper arm.

"Fuck you!" Connor screamed into the night.

Louis held onto him tight." It's Louis. Calm down."

Connor thrashed hard, trying to escape. "Fuck you! Fuck off!"

Now with a firm hold, Louis guided Connor back to the police car. Connor screamed obscenities all the way, doing his best to break free. Louis opened the back door of the police car and flung Connor inside with a little more force than was probably necessary. He took a deep breath and exhaled, ignoring the fact that Connor was now kicking against the window in a rage. It was then that he realised that he had burst the tyre when he had curbed the car.

"Give me fucking strength," he whispered, raising his eyes skywards.

He heard Connor screaming in the back to be let out, accompanied by further thuds on the rear window. It would have been in keeping with the evening for Connor to kick through the glass and shred his major arteries.

Louis opened the front passenger door, stuck his head in and shouted, "Pack that in!"

It was enough to stop Connor for a moment.

Louis slammed the door closed then activated his radio. "X-ray three one, I've located the misper but my tyre's damaged. Can you send recovery and a unit to transport the misper back home?"

"Three-one, that's received. Recovery requested but all units currently engaged."

So, sit tight and shut up, Louis thought to himself grimly. He gave it a moment then got into the driver's seat.

Connor was sat in the back, arms folded and staring at Louis like he had just killed a puppy.

"What are you doing here?" Louis asked, exasperated.

"Mind your own fucking business," Connor snapped back.

"You are my business, you little twit," Louis growled, just about managing to censor himself. "Why would you come here? Don't you know how dangerous it is?"

Connor slammed his hand against the window. "I want to see my mum!"

The vision of the trans child that Luke had described to him flashed in Louis' mind, stuffed unceremoniously between two wheelie bins. He twisted round in his seat. "Fat lot of good for either of you if you end up dead in the process!"

Louis braced himself for the next barrage of abuse. None came. Connor's face crumpled and he burst into tears, sobbing loudly. The sound wrenched at Louis' soul. He opened his mouth to speak but no words came out. It was as if someone had grabbed him by the throat.

"I want my mum!" Connor wailed, tears streaming from his eyes.

Louis wanted to reach for the boy's hand. Connor collapsed back into the seat, crying uncontrollably. His distress was so raw, yet so familiar. Buried deep under the layers of adulthood, Louis' inner child heard Connor's pain and screamed back in a primal show of solidarity. Louis gritted his teeth, willing himself not to cry too.

* * * * *

Louis rubbed his heavy eyes and yawned. It was now six o'clock in the morning and they were still sat on Garnett Street. The stationary police vehicle had frightened off prostitutes and punters alike. He looked over his shoulder. When Connor had finally stopped crying, a wave of exhaustion seemed to hit him. He was now curled up in a foetal position across the back seats, snoring gently.

Louis was sorely tempted to close his eyes for a moment as well but knew that he'd soon be snoring too if he did. Instead, he opened the door gently and stepped out onto the pavement. The air was cold and damp but it did the trick. He stretched then got back into the car.

Connor was awake now and sat up. He yawned and looked outside. "As if we're still here! I could've got an Uber and been in my bed hours ago."

Louis looked back at him and smiled wryly, glad to have the cheeky Connor back. "Maybe you should think about that the next time you decide to go missing."

"I wasn't missing," Connor sighed wearily. "It's my mum that's missing. No one's seen or heard from her in months. No one knows where she is. Why isn't anyone bothered about that apart from me? Don't you think I'd stop coming out to look for her if I knew she was alright?"

They were fair questions, Louis admitted to himself. As he thought about it more, Aliyah had said exactly the same thing about Emma in the professionals meeting. No one could actually confirm that she was safe and well at the moment. Even the Neighbourhood Policing Team hadn't sighted her for a while. He picked up his handheld terminal from the passenger seat and twisted round to face Connor. "Ok then, let's report her missing."

Connor looked at him dubiously.

"Name?"

"Emma Jane McAllen."

"Age?"

"Thirty."

Over the next fifteen minutes, Louis tapped all the details that Connor gave him about Emma into a missing person report. As he came to the end of the form, he asked, "Have you got a picture?"

Connor hesitated for a moment then drew out his phone. He tapped the screen a couple of times then held it up for Louis to see. Emma was an attractive woman but clearly ravaged by long-term drug use. Connor definitely had her eyes. She was sat on a cheap-looking sofa holding a cupcake with a candle in it. Connor was next to her, his face looking younger and softer. Both of them were smiling but there was a sadness etched deep across their faces. Louis zoomed in and took a picture of Emma's face then uploaded it to the police computers. "There. She's officially a missing person."

"Thank you." Connor nodded solemnly and sat back. After a moment, he said, "You were in care, right? You know what it's like?"

"I suppose so," Louis replied. "That isn't an excuse to go missing, by the way."

"If you find my mum, I won't have to," Connor replied. He closed his eyes and leaned his head against the window. "Do you remember your mum?"

"Yeah," said Louis, staring out into the gloom. "Stubborn. Fought with everyone. When they decided to take her into the psychiatric hospital, it took four of them to get her there. She was the best, though, even when she wasn't well."

"Mine too," replied Connor, his eyes still closed. "People said she was a risk to me but that's not true. She just couldn't look after me the same way as other parents. Where's your mum now?"

Louis hesitated. "She's around. I don't see her much."

"How come?" Connor asked.

"We had a massive argument a while back," replied Louis, closing his eyes and rubbing them again. He should have known that a vague answer wouldn't be enough for Connor. "We both said some pretty harsh things. I think we're both waiting for each other to make the first move now."

When he opened his eyes, he saw Connor frowning at him in the rearview mirror. Louis seemed to read his mind. "I know, it probably seems pretty stupid to you when you can't even see your mum. Families, eh?"

They sat in silence for a moment, both of them deep in their own thoughts. Suddenly, something on the road caught Louis' eye. He leaned forward in his seat and gazed outside intently. When he saw it, he whispered urgently to Connor.

"What?" Connor leaned forward though the gap between the seats. He followed Louis' pointed finger then gasped in wonderment.

A large fox stared back at them, the large yellow eyes glinting in the streetlight. Its bushy tail swished cautiously, body tensed in anticipation of having to run for its life. The two of them studied the fox, fascinated by its lithe, elegant form. Solitary and beautiful. It stared at them for a moment longer before darting off into the shadows.

"Didn't I tell you?" Connor whispered. "The city's different at night."

"I guess so," Louis whispered back, still spellbound.

Louis' radio suddenly chirped, startling them both. He answered the point-to-point call from Luke, who told him that they were on the way to collect them. Louis breathed a heavy sigh of relief, more than ready for this set of shifts to end.

* * * * *

Louis sat slumped in a booth in the Winston Pub, shielding his weary eyes from the sunlight that now streamed through the window. Sharlene and Damien were sat opposite and Luke was beside him. Only two officers from full nights had joined them for breakfast at the carvery; they had eaten quickly and headed off, pleading exhaustion. By all accounts, it had been a trying night for everyone.

The recovery truck had arrived shortly after Damien and Luke, allowing them to get Connor back home and then return to the station in good time. Louis had recounted events to Luke, including his decision to report Emma as a missing person. It was a good shout, Luke had said. There could be little criticism for wanting to check on the welfare of a vulnerable woman, even if she did prove difficult to locate. That reassured Louis. The only thing that continued to niggle him was how Connor had come to know about Garnett Street in the first place. Connor had murmured something about Wilko telling him then evaded any further questions about it.

Luke nudged Louis and he tuned back into the conversation about a team night out tomorrow.

"It'll be just what we all need," Luke said. "No excuses, Louis. Me, you and Damo can share a taxi into town since we're all on the same route."

That was news to Louis. He knew Luke lived on a new-build estate ten minutes away from him but hadn't realised Damien was in his neck of the woods too.

"I'll let you know about travel arrangements, mate," Damien said, pulling out his mobile as it chimed. Louis saw a sly smile spread across his face. "I might not be coming from home."

"What is that smile about, Damo?" exclaimed Sharlene.

Damien chuckled to himself but didn't offer any reply. He then excused himself and slid out of the booth, flashing his colleagues a cheeky wink. Sharlene and Luke looked askance at each other for a moment then carried on the conversation.

Louis sipped his coffee, starting to relax a little. It would be good to have a decent night out; the first, in fact, since New Year's Eve.

"Oh my god!" Sharlene hooted and pointed through the window. "Look what he's up to!"

Louis followed her gaze and saw Damien stood in the car park, enjoying a passionate embrace with a young, blonde woman in a purple outdoor jacket. Her hair was tied up in a neat bun and Louis spotted her black patrol boots and cargo trousers.

"That's Amy, the new PCSO who just transferred to Neighbourhood Policing," said Luke, craning his neck over Louis to get a closer look. "Go on, lad!"

"One way to start your shift," murmured Sharlene, then added dreamily, "My man used to kiss me like that in the beginning."

Louis found himself struggling to look away as well. Damien towered over Amy and her slender frame was dwarfed by his massive body, his long muscular arms enveloping her completely as he kissed her. It had been a long while since Louis enjoyed that kind of intimacy.

"What do you reckon, Sharl?" asked Luke, grinning. "A Crunchie Bar says its over by Valentine's Day."

"Yessah," she laughed, slapping him five.

Louis drained his coffee and stood up to go get a refill for everyone, grateful for the excuse to avert his eyes from what was going on outside. He was no prude, but neither did he need any reminders of what his life seemed to be lacking at the moment. He walked round the corner and stood in front of the coffee machine, beginning to make the drinks.

A familiar male voice called out behind him. "PC Mortimer? Louis?"

Louis turned to find Elliott standing behind him. He looked fresh and healthy, dressed in a navy-blue button-down shirt and black jeans. His green eyes shone as he flashed his movie-star smile. He smelt deliciously of some classic Calvin Klein aftershave. For the briefest second, Louis pictured himself kissing Elliott in the car park whilst others looked on enviously. That bubble quickly burst as he suddenly became very conscious of the fact that his face was greasy, his eyes were bloodshot from lack of sleep and he smelt far from fresh.

"Hi, Elliott," he replied, smiling wanly and hoping he didn't have any food in his teeth. "Small world."

"True," said Elliott. The creases around the corners of his eyes appeared as his grin widened. "But you just can't beat the breakfast here, can you? You look like you've had a rough night."

"Our mutual friend has been keeping us busy," said Louis. "He went missing from the home last night and I found him on the red-light district."

Elliott's smile faded to an expression of grave concern. "Is he ok?"

Louis nodded. "I don't know where he got the information from, but he reckoned his mum might be there."

"He's a bright lad. I suppose it was only a matter of time before he worked it out."

Louis nodded in agreement. "He's helped me complete a missing person report for her. Hopefully that will reassure him a little and see that she's located."

"Great idea." Elliott turned as an athletic-looking brunette in blue jeans and a thick black jumper arrived at his side. He put his arm round her shoulders and introduced her. "This is Jane. My umm...girlfriend, I guess. Can I call you that? It's been four months, after all?"

Jane giggled as Elliott kissed the side of her neck and pushed him playfully. "I suppose so."

"She's been up from London for the weekend," Elliott informed Louis. "Just making the most of our time and the awesome breakfast before her train back. Speaking of which…"

They bade Louis goodbye, with Elliott agreeing to give Connor a stern talking-to when he saw him on Monday. Louis watched them leave, hand in hand. He glanced upwards, imploring whatever heavenly power that might exist to either strike him down or allow the ground to swallow him. Giving himself a mental shake, he gathered up the drinks and returned to the table.

Luke put his arm round Louis' shoulders and playfully ruffled his hair, "Bad luck, pal."

Sharlene cocked her eyebrow.

"Louis is hot for teacher," Luke chuckled.

Louis shrugged him off. "Ignore him, Sharl. He's had too many knocks to the head on the rugby pitch."

"True," she said, watching Elliott depart. "But damn, look at that bum. I feel seh mi hot fi teacher too."

Luke grabbed her hand dramatically. "Oh, Sharl, I love it when you speak patois."

Sharlene kissed her teeth and drained her coffee. "Right, lads. I'm off home. See you tomorrow night."

Louis and Luke did the same and followed her out into the car park. Damien and Amy were still in the same spot, kissing without any sign of stopping.

"Jesus, Damo!" Luke shouted over at them. "Either put her down or get a bloody room. This is a family establishment!"

Damien paused long enough to extend his arm and give Luke the finger, then returned his attention to Amy. Louis slid into his car and set it in motion, doing his best not to look at Damien as he drove past.

CHAPTER 10

Sunday had come and gone in a blur. Louis had slept through until past lunchtime, unusual for him. By the time he had woken up, the sky outside was darkening. He had given a frustrated groan when he looked at the time. That was most of his rest-day gone. The only one who didn't have a problem with the lie-in was Gonzo, who seemed to relish having his human home to snuggle into.

Determined to make something of the day, Louis went for a run then set about various domestic chores that were neglected during his working week. Periodically, he brooded on his encounter with Elliott. He felt stupid for thinking Elliott might have been interested in him.

Right on cue, memories of Simon wheedled their way into his thoughts. They had been together for two years, splitting up just before Louis joined the force. Louis thought of it as his first proper adult relationship. Simon was older than him, which Louis had liked. There was a worldliness about him, not least because he was a therapist. They had met through Louis' work as a housing support officer for people with mental health problems; he would escort one of his clients to Simon's office once a week for a session.

He was the first person that Louis had felt comfortable enough to talk about his family background with. Simon listened attentively, offering insights into how Louis' childhood may have shaped him as an adult. Over time, the insights began to come with more of an edge. If Louis didn't like something or didn't want to go somewhere, it was something to do with his trauma.

Reflecting on it now, Louis supposed that the relationship had been controlling. Never any violence, but controlling all the same. He didn't see it at the time. Simon became moody and more distant, which only made Louis try harder to reach him. The final straw was Louis' decision to apply for the police. Simon accused him of wanting out of their relationship, that he would inevitably end up cheating with all and sundry at work.

That went on for weeks. Louis had finished the application almost as soon as the recruitment window opened but had held off submitting it, weighing up whether a job was worth wrecking his relationship for. After one particularly acrimonious dinner, where Simon mused on Louis' need to control other people due to having so little control of his own life growing up, Louis stomped into the bedroom to his laptop and clicked send.

When he told Simon what he had done the following day, Simon wept quietly and pleaded with Louis to explain why he wasn't enough for him? Was sex with other men so important? He left Louis' flat and drove off, the last time Louis would see him.

The break-up came by e-mail a few days later. It was practically a thesis on all of Louis' shortcomings and hang-ups. Too needy. Compulsively drawing people in and then pushing them away when the attention became too overwhelming. Obsessed with physical intimacy as a distraction from forming meaningful emotional connections. Louis read and re-read each paragraph with a hand over his mouth, mortified. The e-mail reminded him of the day he had, as an adult, sat down in the Social Services archive to read through the files they had kept on him.

And in any case, Simon had concluded, the police were at odds with his anti-oppressive values. He couldn't be in a relationship with someone who would so readily join an organisation that was so prejudiced to ethnic minorities and the LGBTQ+ community simply due to a neurotic need for power over others.

The realisation came to Louis in the middle of his foundation training as the guest lecturer from a domestic abuse charity explained the concept of controlling and coercive behaviour. He sat in his seat, pen in mouth, as every frame of reference he had for the relationship shattered. From that moment, he understood on an intellectual level that he wasn't at fault; but Simon's parting words nonetheless hooked into a deeper belief that Louis wasn't good enough and that's why people inevitably left him.

Now standing in front of his mirror in the spare bedroom, buttoning up a dark green cotton shirt, Louis ruminated on that thought. Gonzo strutted in and brushed himself up against Louis' legs, leaving behind wisps of fur on the ankles of his black jeans. Louis picked the heavy cat up and cradled him in the crook of his arm like a baby, scratching under his chin. "Everyone except you, mate."

He set Gonzo down and dusted himself off, also spritzing himself with some Paco Rabanne. He checked his watch. Twelve o'clock on the dot. Team outings started early in the day to take full advantage of time. Luke had messaged to say he wasn't far off in the taxi now. Louis took a final look in the mirror, smiled sheepishly at himself then headed downstairs to wait.

* * * * *

Aliyah strode into Martin's office and sat down in one of the chairs in front of his desk. The building would have been considered modern in the nineties but, two decades on, it was sorely in need of a facelift. Dotted on the greying walls of Martin's office were posters regarding various safeguarding issues. Martin had a corner desk with his computer screen up against the wall, allowing him an unobstructed view when someone came to speak to him. Boxes of files were stacked along the walls, making the already-small room feel more claustrophobic.

Martin had been typing furiously when Aliyah walked in but spun round in his chair to face her. "Let me guess. Connor?"

Aliyah nodded gravely. "I just finished on the phone with the manager from Robin Hill. He went out with the two other residents over the weekend and did a runner. The police picked him up in the early hours hanging around on Garnett Street."

"The red-light district," Martin said, confirming he had understood the reference this time.

"I'm worried about him," said Aliyah. "He told the police that he'd heard from some rough sleeper that his mum might be living around there. It's so dangerous, Martin. He's putting himself at serious risk."

Martin took off his black, chunky-framed glasses and gave the lenses a wipe as he considered what Aliyah was saying. "And are we reasonably certain that it's the only reason he's going up there? No indication that he's being sexually exploited? I know one of the residents at Robin Hill has a history of selling sex. Is there a chance he's influencing Connor?"

Aliyah shook her head. "No, I'm not seeing any other indicators.

Connor doesn't smoke or use drugs. He'll have a bit of alcohol if it's there but he doesn't deliberately seek it out. He's good with his money. He's actually the only kid on my caseload that saves his cash."

"Relationships? Girlfriend, boyfriend, that kind of thing?"

"Nope. He's a lone wolf. It's not something he talks about, to be honest. Elliott and I did a bit of direct work with him around safer relationships and safer sex a while ago. He didn't let anything slip either way. Called us a pair of weirdos and asked for a hot chocolate."

Martin laughed. "Isn't it refreshing to have a teenager with a bit of innocence still about them. I only hope I can say the same for my two when the time comes."

Aliyah followed the gesture of his hand to a primary school photo on the wall of his two sons. She smiled. Martin was a good team manager, always calm with an air of professional wisdom about him.

"Did he stay put last night?"

"Yes," Aliyah replied. "The staff watched him like hawks all day."

She paused for a moment, gathering her thoughts, before venturing, "Martin, should we be thinking of securing him?"

"Absolutely not," replied Martin, shaking his head emphatically.

"This can't go on, though!" Aliyah raised her voice as she realised just how worried she was for Connor. Worried enough to consider going to court and asking for an order to have Connor placed in a locked children's home on welfare grounds.

"I agree," said Martin, unfazed. He was used to having

impassioned case discussions with Aliyah. "But I used to apply for secure orders a lot when I worked in London. They're nigh-on impossible to get, even in cases where the child really should be somewhere secure. A judge wouldn't entertain it for Connor, not for a minute."

"I know, I know," Aliyah conceded, sighing. Actually, it was a relief to hear Martin rule it out as an option. The very thought of locking Connor away somewhere broke her heart. "I wouldn't want to see him in a secure unit either. I feel awful for even thinking it. I just don't know what to do with him."

Aliyah reeled off the current interventions she had put in place, also mentioning that Louis had reported Emma missing on Connor's behalf. Martin nodded approvingly.

"And Elliott has offered to go up to Robin Hill during the day to do educational inputs with him. He felt it might be safer for Connor not to travel to school for the time being, until we can be more reassured that he won't go missing."

"That's going to be a little claustrophobic for him," Martin observed. "All day, every day stuck in the children's home."

"Elliott's on it," Aliyah said with a smile. "He's planning field trips, the lot. And I can guarantee you, he's the one person that Connor won't run off from. To be fair, Elliott could outrun Connor without breaking a sweat."

Martin returned her smile. "Connor certainly has a good team of professionals working around him. Elliott seems very dedicated. Has he said anything more about applying for Special Guardianship?"

"I gave him the information the other day" replied Aliyah. "He hasn't said anymore since then. We've agreed not to say anything to Connor until Elliott's made his mind up."

"I think that's wise."

"Yes." Aliyah clasped her hands together, almost as if she were praying. "I really hope he decides to do it. They have such a good relationship. It could be really positive for Connor."

Martin nodded. "Keep me posted. In the meantime, I'll get in touch with Kirsty at Robin Hill. I'll authorise some extra funding for her to bring in an additional staff member per shift so Connor's got one-to-one support. We'll try that for a fortnight and see how it goes."

Aliyah nodded gratefully and returned to the main office.

* * * * *

Connor sat at the dining table at Robin Hill, propping his head up in his left hand as he idly doodled on the biology worksheet in front of him. Elliott sat adjacent to him, doing his best to keep him motivated.

"I don't know why I need to learn this shit," muttered Connor. "The human digestive system. Food goes in your mouth and..."

"And it's part of the syllabus," Elliott finished the sentence before Connor could. "Come on, Connor. We're nearly done."

"Fine." He filled in the answers with no difficulty. "How come you haven't bollocked me yet for going out on Saturday?"

Elliott shook his head wearily. "Would it make a difference?"

Connor shrugged and smiled innocently. Elliott seemed to be in a weird mood. "Anyway, that copper Louis reported my mum missing. They're going to look for her now. Maybe I'll get to see her soon."

"That would be great if you did," replied Elliott. "It might take a while though. She probably won't be at the top of their list, particularly whilst kids like you are going missing."

"I told Louis I wouldn't," said Connor, starting to doodle on the worksheet again.

"You seem to get on well with Louis," Elliott observed, taking the worksheet from Connor and putting it in his bag before he graffitied it further.

"Yeah, he's sound," Connor replied, yawning. "For a copper, anyway. We were chatting all sorts of shit on Saturday night while we were waiting for the tow truck to come. His mum got sectioned when he was a kid. That's how he ended up in care.""

"Oh right. I suppose he can relate to you pretty well then?"

Connor nodded and was about to say something else but stopped himself. Elliott had started looking a little impatient.

"I'm not sure Louis would want you repeating things about his personal life to everyone."

"Well, you're not *everyone*," Connor replied with a wide grin. "Did I tell you we saw a fox close up too?"

"Since when are you into nature?"

Connor shrugged. "I'm not. But this was cool."

"The city's full of them," said Elliott. "Come to think of it, there used to be some dens up in the woods near here. My dad used to take me camping around there. Go grab a coat and we can have a wander up to see if there's any still there."

Finally, Connor thought, a chance for some fresh air. He leapt to his feet but, before he could leave, Elliott caught his arm gently.

"You never said who told you your mum was living near Garnett Street. Who was it? And don't give me that crap about Wilko."

Connor dropped his gaze. He wanted to tell Elliott that Emma had been texting him. In all fairness, Elliott would probably be the only one to help make sure Connor got to see her. He had given Louis the number she had been using but never said that she had been messaging him recently. He reluctantly decided not to tell Elliott. He would have to tell the staff and Aliyah, and they would probably want to do some assessment to make sure Emma was ok before they allowed that kind of contact. In other words, the line of communication would be effectively cut off. "It was Wilko. He'd seen her in town and she told him."

Elliott seemed to accept that. He still had hold of Connor's forearm. "Listen, I wasn't going to mention this until things had settled down a little. I've been talking to Aliyah about the possibility of looking after you instead of you being in a children's home."

Connor frowned. This news was totally left-field. "You mean like a foster carer?"

"Not exactly," Elliott replied. "More like an adoption. You wouldn't be a Looked-After Child anymore. No more social workers, no more reviews, no more police-checks every time you want to sleep over at a mate's house. I'd basically be your parent."

Connor's frown deepened. This was too much to process. Elliott squeezed his arm reassuringly, "I know it's a lot to spring on you. I've been thinking about it for a while. Aliyah and I were going to talk to you about it because obviously you have to be on board too. But none of it can happen if you're putting yourself at risk all the time. The court will think I won't be able to keep you safe."

Connor bit his lip. "I hear you."

"Come on," said Elliott, standing up. "Grab your stuff and we'll go for that walk. We can talk more about it then."

Connor nodded and flew up the stairs two steps at a time. Today was shaping up a lot differently to what he'd anticipated.

CHAPTER 11

"Hurry up, Louis!" Sharlene stood with her arms folded, scowling. She was flanked by Luke and Damien.

"I'm going as fast as I can," Louis mumbled, his mouth full of pitta bread and chicken.

It was approaching ten o'clock and they were the last people standing. After finishing their drinks in the last pub, Luke and Sharlene had insisted on taking Louis to the city's gay village. Never mind that Elliott! Sharlene had exclaimed. This had prompted Damien to ask who Elliott was, leading to Luke recounting the events in the carvery.

"You missed it," Luke had said, slurring his words a little, "Because you were tickling Amy's tonsils with your tongue."

Sharlene had cackled at that, slapping her hand on the table.

"Aye, alright then," Damien had said, tipping the last of his pint down his throat. "Let's see if we can't get Louis' tonsils tickled a wee bit too."

Luke and Sharlene had cheered. Louis had shaken his head in disbelief, blushing and gathering up his jacket before following them out of the pub.

Now they stood outside a kebab shop, lining their stomachs for the next round. It had been a good night. Everyone was merrily drunk, recounting old war stories and gently taking the piss out of each other. Louis was just happy to sit back, relaxed in their company, and let the gossip and bawdy jokes wash over him. Even Damien was uncharacteristically sociable, his Glaswegian accent growing more pronounced the more he drank.

Louis found it funny seeing everyone in their normal clothes, like when kids bumped into their teachers in the supermarket. Sharlene looked glamourous in heels and a little black dress with her braids down; her complaints of being cold received no sympathy. Damien eventually relented and let her borrow his black leather jacket. He was wearing a red short-sleeve shirt and skin-tight black jeans that made it clear to anyone who looked that he put the hours in at the gym. His hair had been freshly cut and his face shaved, courtesy of a new Turkish barber that had opened near home. Luke was wearing dark blue jeans and a black cotton jumper, accessorised simply by a chunky silver chain. His five o'clock shadow gave him a rugged look.

Louis finally finished his food and they continued on to Mama Kofi's Show Bar. They entered via the big red double-doors and looked around. It was pretty busy to say that it was only Monday. There were drag queens serving behind the bar and otherwise circulating throughout the venue.

"Hello, sailor!" Louis looked round just in time to see a slender drag queen dressed in white with a peroxide blonde beehive wig wrap her arms round Damien's neck. She kicked her legs up into the air for him to catch her. "My hero! To the bar please, darling."

Damien looked over at them, shrugged his shoulders and wandered off with the flamboyant snow-queen in his arms.

116

"That man!" Sharlene yelled over the music into Louis' ear. "Look at him!"

Louis followed her gaze. Damien was stood at the bar surrounded by four drag queens. Seemingly at their behest, he flexed his biceps on one arm while they took selfies with him.

Luke reappeared, carrying four pints of lager. "Cheap beer, quick service, eighties music, this place has got it all!"

He spotted Damien in the distance with the drag queens fawning over him and pulled his phone out to take a photo. "There's one for the team Whatsapp!"

At Sharlene's insistence, they finished their drinks quickly so she could lead them onto the dancefloor. At that point, Louis finally relaxed and started to dance as the familiar opening chords from Blondie's 'Call Me' rang out across the bar.

* * * * *

Connor was sprawled out across one of the sofas in the living room, half-watching Deadpool on the TV. Thanks to good behaviour, they'd managed to negotiate a slightly later bedtime tonight with the staff. Jimmy and Ariana were snuggled up to each other on another sofa. Connor still couldn't quite work out what the deal was with them. They didn't seem to be in a typical boyfriend-girlfriend type of relationship. Maybe friends with benefits? No. They were more like kindred spirits, happy to have found each other.

He felt his phone buzz in his pocket and he pulled it out. He gritted his teeth to stop himself from crying out with joy. A message from Emma.

"CJ, u ok?"

He texted back quickly. "Yh. U?"

"No. Police av been ringing this phone. Did u tell some1?"

Shit! He paused for a moment then replied, "Asked police 2 find u."

The three flickering dots that appeared, signifying that Emma was typing a new message, seemed to stay there forever. Finally, the response came and Connor's heart sank. "Shouldn't av done that love. Need 2 avoid police atm. Guna need 2 lay low 4 abit."

Connor felt prickles running up the back of his neck. "Need 2cu mam!"

He slid his phone surreptitiously down the side of the couch cushion as a member of late staff came into the room carrying three bowls of popcorn. She handed one to Connor, one to Ariana and Jimmy and kept one for herself. He couldn't remember her name. She was a plump little thing in her early twenties. Ariana said that she was an agency worker, not a full-time member of the staff team. That figured, Connor thought. She didn't seem to know much in the way of the home's routines.

Once he was happy that she was engrossed in the film, Connor drew out his phone again and looked at the screen. Emma had replied. "Can u come 2nite? Will av 2go dn south asap so police dnt get me."

"Where 2meet?"

"Garnett St."

Connor opened up the internet browser on his phone to check some information. He did some quick calculations. He could make it but he'd need to work fast. "OK coming now."

He ate his popcorn as quickly as possible then stood up and walked over to the staff member. He showed her his empty bowl and said, "Please could I get some more from the kitchen, miss?"

She smiled and nodded. "Of course you can. You've bolted that down!"

"I'm a growing boy, miss," replied Connor with a cheeky grin, puffing his chest out for effect. "Can I get you anything, miss?"

"No, thanks."

Connor called over to Jimmy and Ariana to see if they wanted anything. The last thing he needed was them creating drama. Both shook their heads and carried on watching the movie. He took a few steps in the direction of the kitchen then paused and called back, "Is the kitchen locked, miss?"

"No, it's still open," she replied, not looking round.

Perfect.

He entered the kitchen quietly, taking care to check if the other two lates staff were milling around. There was no one about. Connor figured that they were in the office chatting. He checked his pockets. He had his inhaler, bus pass and a few pounds along with his charging cable. He was wearing a black Nike tracksuit; not ideal for going out in this cold, damp weather but he couldn't risk changing his clothes. He spotted a black beanie hat in the empty fruit basket on the worktop. He grabbed it and slid it on his head, pulling it down around his ears.

Connor paused for a minute. He'd promised Louis he wouldn't do this again. To be fair to Louis, he had kept his word about everything he'd said he would do, so it felt bad to betray his trust. Elliott also came to mind. He'd been clear that going missing would only make it harder for him to apply to be Connor's guardian. Connor still wasn't sure how he felt about that, but he certainly didn't want to rule it out. There was so much to lose.

He shook his head, bringing fresh resolve. Emma was his mum. He had to see her. He looked at his phone. Five-past ten. Go time.

He pushed the bar on the fire exit door and it opened softly. He slipped out and closed the door silently. Rather than following the path round to the front and triggering the security light, he ran up the grass embankment towards the conifer hedges that bordered the home. He skulked along the tree-line carefully, feeling water seep into his trainers as he squelched through the muddy ground. When he reached the driveway entrance, he turned towards the building to make sure no one happened to be looking out of the windows.

Connor ran full tilt from the driveway downhill to the bus stop. As he crossed the road, he could see the bus approaching in the distance. A moment later, he was sat at the back of the empty bus heading towards the city. The perfect crime, he thought gloomily.

He plugged his phone into the USB port on the seat in front of him and began to charge his phone whilst he messaged Emma. "On the bus."

The reply came in seconds. "OK love. Read this careful."

A moment later, a more detailed message came through, explaining what Connor needed to do when he arrived at Garnett Street. A final message followed: "Cnt wait 2cu CJ, miss u so much."

It was too soon to get excited. Connor clenched his right hand into a fist and squeezed whilst trying to slow down his breathing. Elliott had taught him that. Once more, he felt a terrible pang of guilt for letting Louis and Elliott down; but it had to be done. He looked out of the window into the dark, wet night with a grim expression on his face.

* * * * *

The crowd in Mama Kofi's had steadily increased. The vast majority of revellers seemed to be students from the local university. The dancefloor was heaving, the crowd egged on every so often by one of the drag queens ascending to the stage to perform a song.

Louis had been dancing with Luke and Sharlene for ages, both of whom looked like they were having the time of their lives. To his left, Louis spotted a guy dancing with a mixed group. He was cute in a nerdy sort of way with straight brown hair, square black glasses and a Wolverine T-shirt that clung to his skinny frame. Their two groups began to merge into one larger circle, bringing Louis face-to-face with him. He smiled shyly and Louis reciprocated. Sharlene gave Louis a not-so-surreptitious wink and a wide grin.

Before she could embarrass him further, she was distracted by the opening bars of The B52s' 'Loveshack'. She screamed excitedly at Luke, who had somehow become covered in glitter at some point during the night and now shimmered like a disco-ball.

As the crowd surged, Louis and Wolverine T-shirt were jostled close together. He put his hand on Louis' shoulder, drawing him down a little so he could introduce himself as Sam. They began dancing more in sync with each other, exchanging smiles and the occasional touch of the hand.

Just then, Louis spotted Damien across the room in a darker corner of the bar. He was sipping a pint but looking straight at

Louis, his eyes dark. Louis wondered whether he should wave him over to join them. No. Damien had a strange expression on his face, like he was studying Louis intently. He wondered if this was what animals in the wild felt like when they were being watched by a predator.

The touch of Sam's hand on his brought Louis' attention back to his new dance partner. The song finished and the floor began to clear a little. Sam signalled that he was going to the toilet. Louis gave him a thumbs-up and pointed to the bar.

They parted ways and Louis ordered himself a pint. Damien was nowhere to be seen now. Louis wiped the sweat from his brow, suddenly realising how hot he was. He headed to the door that led to the outside beer garden. The cold air swept over his face, providing welcome relief.

"Having a good night?"

Louis turned and saw Damien stood under a patio heater that resembled a giant black umbrella. Damien's voice wasn't unfriendly but the joviality from earlier in the night was no longer there. Louis joined him under the heater. The orange glow from above served to accentuate his handsome chiselled features. Damien was wearing his jacket now, causing the scents of leather and aftershave to mingle into something altogether more delicious.

"Yeah," replied Louis. "Are you?"

"Aye," Damien replied laconically, sipping his pint. "I'm going to finish this and get going though."

"If you wait, I'll round up those two and we can grab a taxi together," said Louis.

He and Damien turned to look through the glass doors as the crowd cheered. Mama Kofi herself had taken to the stage to perform Belinda Carlisle's 'Nobody Owns Me'. Sharlene was singing her heart out and Luke was doing something that resembled air guitar.

"Nah, let them enjoy themselves," said Damien. "They need to blow off some steam. I might not be going home anyway."

Luke nodded, remembering Amy the PCSO, and took a larger sip of his drink. He was starting to feel uncomfortable. Being this close to Damien, there was no escape from the steely gaze of those dark-blue eyes. Louis started to notice the finer details of his face: the slight dimple in the middle of his chin, a faded scar just under his right eyebrow, the delicate curve of the Cupid's Bow of his upper lip.

The bow flexed and Louis realised Damien was smiling now. "What happened to your nerdy little friend?"

Sam had become a distant memory. He managed to reply, "Gents, I think."

Damien nodded and downed the rest of his pint. "I'm away, pal. Enjoy the rest of your night."

Louis nodded, realising he was staring into Damien's eyes still. He jumped as he felt Damien's hand press up against the small of his back. For a split-second, he thought he was falling and Damien was catching him.

Damien drew Louis closer and kissed him slowly on the lips. He stopped a moment later and moved his head back slightly, leaving just millimetres between their lips. Louis' exhausted, intoxicated brain couldn't process what was happening.

The first instinct was to push Damien away in shock. Louis fought past that instinct and brought his lips back to Damien's. Damien kissed Louis again with a delicious softness that Louis would never have credited to this brute. The tips of their tongues touched, giving him the sensation of electricity flashing up and down his spine. He could feel the warmth of Damien's body against his now. He wanted Damien to draw him in closer and not let go.

And then it was over. Damien pulled back abruptly and released him from his arms. Louis blinked hard.

"I'd better go," murmured Damien. He stepped back, turned and walked off in the direction of the doors.

It took a moment for everything to register. What the fuck had just happened? Louis hurried back into the bar but was too late. He saw Damien's broad frame leaving through the front door.

Louis sensed someone hovering behind him and turned round. Sam stood there, shuffling from foot to foot awkwardly.

"I'm sorry," he said. "I umm... didn't realise you were with someone."

"I'm not," Louis replied. "I'm not sure what just happened there."

"Oh. Well, we're moving onto another bar. See you around, I guess?"

Sam didn't wait for a response and darted off back to his friends. It probably looked too much like drama to him, thought Louis. He stood there trying to organise his thoughts. The world around him seemed to slow down. The intense excitement from a moment ago was fading, leaving him overwhelmed by feelings of confusion and rejection. Louis stood in the middle of the bar alone, staring at the front doors in bewilderment.

* * * * *

Connor cocked his head up at the sound of an approaching car. His eyes darted left to right as he gazed from one end of Garnett Street to the other. Nothing came. He sighed heavily and leaned back against the junction box where he had met the woman from the other night. He'd seen a few other women skulking back and forth in the hour he had been waiting here. None of them looked familiar, and yet their emaciated bodies and desperately weary eyes reminded him of his mum.

He pulled his phone out and checked it again. It was well past midnight now and still nothing. Emma had said she was coming for him. He was fighting every rational voice in his head that told him she was going to let him down again. She would come. He dialled her number, heard the electronic voice tell him Emma's phone was switched off. He swore quietly and lowered his head onto his forearms in some pseudo-prayer. She would come.

He jerked up quickly. Footsteps. The click-click of high heels on the pavement. A figure in the distance. Blonde, curly hair, a white blouse, black leather jacket, skinny blue jeans and black knee-high high-heeled boots. He strained to see but it was too dark to make out her face.

"Mam," he gasped, unable to find enough of his voice to call out to her properly.

He wheeled round as the pavement was suddenly bathed in light. A sleek grey Volvo had pulled up beside him. A warm gust of bubblegum-scented air wafted out as the driver's window slid down. Connor blinked in confusion at the thick-lipped white man in glasses.

"CJ? I'm Bryan," he said. "I'm a friend of Emma's. She sent me to get you."

Connor frowned. He glanced back at the woman approaching him. It was his friend from last night. Fuck! "Where is she?"

"At my house," replied Bryan impatiently. "We need to hurry, CJ. There isn't much time."

Connor needed only a second more to make his decision. He hurried round to the front passenger seat and jumped in, pulling on his seatbelt. Bryan set off fast, the tyres screeching as he tore out of Garnett Street's inky blackness.

CHAPTER 12

Louis had finally gotten Luke and Sharlene into a taxi shortly after Damien left, despite their protests that the night was just starting. It was a different story once they were in the taxi. After a few minutes of singing ABBA's 'Dancing Queen', they leaned towards each other and fell into a drunken half-sleep. Louis kept his eye on them in the rearview mirror as the taxi drove them to Sharlene's house first.

After depositing her in the arms of her amused husband, Louis' house was the next stop. In Luke's current state, Louis didn't want to leave him in the taxi by himself. He paid the driver and hauled Luke out of the taxi into his house. They made it into the spare room and Louis lowered Luke onto the bed, pulled his boots off then tucked him under the duvet. He darted back down to the kitchen and returned with a pint of water. Luke was already on his side, snuggling into the pillow with a dreamy expression on his face.

"Night, mate," said Louis, switching off the light.

"Goodnight, god bless," Luke giggled without opening his eyes, making two kissy noises before falling silent.

Louis grinned, switched off the bedroom light and left the door slightly ajar so the hallway light could give the room a fraction of illumination. He crossed over the hallway into his room, where Gonzo had already taken up his position on the left side of the bed near the pillow.

Louis stripped off his clothes quickly and got into the black vest and plaid cotton bottoms he used as pyjamas. He slipped into bed and sighed with relief. After switching off the beside light, he sent Annie a message via Facebook to let her know Luke was with him. She acknowledged the message with a laughing emoji and a meme of a drunken cartoon character.

The last of his duties done, Louis returned in his mind to Mama Kofi's back yard. Damien's arms wrapped around him, his soft full lips locking with Louis'. The way his eyes would close for a moment, as if he was savouring Louis, then flutter open again to drink in more of him. Louis shuddered with the intensity of the memory.

On impulse, he checked Damien's Facebook page. They weren't friends so there was nothing for Louis to see. Not that he expected Damien to have put on a status update telling everyone that he had just kissed a guy from work in a drag bar. Louis snorted mirthlessly at the thought. He wasn't naïve. Of course, he knew there were bisexual guys out there. It was just....Damien?

Another idea sprung to mind. He opened the team Whatsapp group, found Damien's number from the contact list and opened up a private message window to him. His first draft told Damien that they had got home safely. He deleted that and instead asked whether Damien had gotten back ok. The final effort was saying it had been a great night, followed by a number of party-related emojis. Louis groaned and deleted it. Damien's profile picture, a close-up photo of him somewhere sunny wearing black Aviators and a seductive smirk, stared back at Louis.

Whatsapp told Louis that Damien had been last seen half an hour ago. Thoughts of him now together with Amy started to intrude. Why did he stop kissing me? Louis wondered. On cue, the mental box where he kept all of Simon's criticisms and put-downs sprung open to answer the question. Louis stared hard at Damien's photo, almost feeling the scratch of his stubble against his face again. He slapped his phone down onto the bedside table with a frustrated growl and turned onto his left side, squeezing his eyes shut. Gonzo's steady purr lulled him to sleep.

* * * * *

It was around lunchtime when Luke finally surfaced and came padding down the stairs. Louis was laid on the couch watching TV and laughed when he saw the state of him. "You know you're still covered in glitter, right?"

Luke wiped a hand across his forehead, looked at his palm and grunted, "Fuck's sake."

He sank heavily into the adjacent sofa.

Louis got up and returned momentarily with coffees for both of them. Luke accepted his gratefully. "Thanks for putting me up. I messaged Annie and she's coming to get me."

"No problem," replied Louis. "What are you doing with the rest of the day?"

"Meh. Gym, shower, parenting. It's some sort of staff training day today so the girls aren't at school. You?"

"Pretty much the same. Apart from the parenting, obviously."

Luke nodded. "Good times last night, eh? Where did Damo get to?"

129

"Not sure," Louis shrugged. He desperately wanted to tell Luke what had happened between them, if for no other reason than to convince himself that it wasn't a figment of his imagination. The only thing that stopped him was the thought that Damien might not want his colleagues to know. "He left just before us. Said he wasn't going home."

"Dirty dog," Luke chuckled.

Louis couldn't resist probing. "You and Sharl are always saying that about him. Is he a bit of a player?"

"Not exactly. Put it this way, he gets plenty of attention from the opposite sex and he's not shy of it." Luke sipped his coffee then added, "Plenty of attention from the same sex, come to think of it. I mean, you've seen him, right? Wouldn't you?"

Louis spluttered as his mouthful of coffee went down the wrong way.

"Easy, pal!" Luke laughed. "That was out of order, sorry."

"No, no," Louis gasped, trying to recovery himself. "It's fine."

"Damo's a good lad," said Luke earnestly. "He comes across as a grumpy bastard but he'd be the first to back you up if you needed help. He just needs the right person to come along and tie him down, I suppose."

Louis was grateful for the knock at the front door and sprang up to answer it. Annie and the kids were on the doorstep.

"They wanted to say hi to you," she said, smiling.

"Hi, Louis!" both girls cried in unison.

Ordinaily, it would be cute. Right now, it was like nails down a blackboard. Louis smiled weakly. "Hi girls. Come in."

They dashed past him and straight onto Luke's lap, hugging him. He reciprocated just as excitedly, flung them over his shoulders and carried them upstairs with him, telling Annie he was just getting his things.

"I hope his snoring didn't keep you awake," said Annie.

Louis shook his head and offered her some coffee, which she declined.

"Oh, by the way. My mate was Night DC yesterday. Apparently, that lad you've been dealing with lately did a runner from his care home again last night."

"Shit." The force ran a skeleton crew of detectives overnight. Their role was to monitor any serious logs and co-ordinate the appropriate response. Missing children fell under their purview. "Where did they find him?"

"They haven't yet," Annie replied. "The duty DI's declared him a high-risk MISPER. Telecoms say his phone left the network around midnight and no-one's been able to reach him since. No social media activity, nothing. Keep your phone handy. They're giving it another couple of hours then they're going to start offering out overtime to anyone who wants to help search. I figured you'd want to be involved so I gave them your name."

They were interrupted by Luke bustling down the stairs with the girls.

"Your cat's so fluffy, Louis!" exclaimed Polly.

"I hope he wasn't mean to you," smiled Louis. Gonzo was generally quite patient with people but small children made him a little skittish.

She shook her head. Luke put his hands on the girls' backs and steered them towards the door. Annie followed them out, leaving Luke to bid goodbye to Louis. After he shut the front door, Louis made a mental plan of action. A run, then a hot shower to clear his head. He'd prep some food so he was ready to go in the event of a call to help search for Connor.

* * * * *

Louis milled around the briefing room chatting to two of his friends from training school. Noreen was a slight, bubbly young Pakistani woman of around twenty-two. She took great pleasure in the fact that her job put off most of the potential suitors her family introduced her to. Louis had met her parents at the attestation ceremony, where their cohort had taken the Oath of Constable. They were quiet, dignified people who seemed proud and worried for their daughter in equal measure.

Jack was older than Noreen, closer to Louis' age. Stocky and blond with permanently rosy cheeks, the only thing he had talked about throughout the last year was his plan to join the Roads Policing Team as soon as he could. He was straightforward, reliable and could regurgitate traffic law ad nauseum.

It seemed they were the only three who had volunteered for the overtime. Louis had gotten the phone call at around three o'clock, asking him to get to his nearest station for a remote briefing at six o'clock. It was five-to six now.

He turned his head at the sound of the door opening and saw Damien walking over to them. Louis felt his heart quicken and his mouth go dry. He was annoyed at himself for the reaction. Of course he would have eventually run into Damien again. He just hadn't expected it to be so soon.

Damien joined the trio, towering over the them. He stood next to

Louis but didn't offer any particularly different greeting; no-one would have guessed that they'd spent last night out drinking together. There was a brooding air about him that felt dangerous but intriguing; like watching dark-blue thunderclouds rolling in across the sky. The smell of his crisp, cool aftershave filled Louis' nostrils, taking him right back to their kiss.

"Hi, Damien," said Noreen coyly, a wide smile spreading across her face.

If Louis could have gotten away with it, he would have kicked her in the ankle. What had Luke been saying earlier about Damien not being short of attention from the opposite sex?

Jack was excited to see Damien for an entirely different reason. "Ay up, Damo! Got my traffic attachment coming up next month, at last!"

Damien nodded. "Nice one, mate. You'll be sporting one of these before long."

He tapped at his black tac-vest. Luke had explained a while back that specialist Ops units like Roads Policing were issued different kit. Damien had evidently done a stint with them. Despite the cold weather, he was wearing short sleeves. Louis tried not to linger too much on the memory of those long, muscular arms wrapped round him. He broke away from the group and tried to make himself useful by turning on the monitor and activating the Teams app. Someone had already started the briefing so he joined it then sat down with the others.

Detective Inspector Ramini introduced himself, speaking with a southern accent. He was sat at the head of a conference table somewhere in another part of the force, joined by a mixture of uniformed and plain-clothes officers. The conferencing equipment fitted in each briefing room allowed him to see and hear the people dialling in, and vice-versa. He ran through the circumstances of Connor's disappearance, the timeline so far and the enquiries that needed to be done next. Louis glanced over at Damien, who was sat furthest away from him on the row. His jaw tightened as he jotted details down in his pocket notebook, emphasising his chiselled features.

"Weaver's Yard folks." Louis' attention snapped back to the screen as Inspector Ramini addressed them. "For now, patrol the city centre and see if you spot him. Recent intel suggests that he's hanging around with street drinkers and rough sleepers, so give them a rattle and see what they know. Damo, I'll leave you to deploy the troops on that end."

Ramini ran through a few more details then concluded the briefing. Once the screen went dead, Damien stood up. "Jack, grab your Taser. You and Noreen can go out together and Louis can come with me."

"Gotcha," said Jack a little glumly. Probably disappointed not to be in a car with Damien to talk about Roads Policing.

Once more, Louis felt like he was in a tailspin. He'd half-expected Damien to avoid him, given how offhand he'd been with him so far. In spite of the inner turmoil, he held up a pair of car-keys for a patrol car and asked, "Peugeot ok?"

Damien gave him a wry smile and nodded. All the response drivers liked the Peugeots best. "Louis and I will head up to Garnett Street and patrol round that area. You guys head to City Square. Let's look to meal about ten at the Maccies in the retail park."

The plan agreed, everyone headed out to the car park to claim their vehicles. After stashing their kit bags in the boot, Louis and

Damien got into the car. Damien started the engine and guided the car smoothly towards the front gate. The silence was uncomfortable. Desperate to find some way to break it, Louis activated his radio and called out to the operator, "4029."

"4029," a male operator responded, using Louis' collar number to confirm he was talking to him.

"4029, show me with 2201. Single-crewed taser unit. We're deploying to search for this high-risk MISPER."

"All received, 4029. Good hunting."

"There was a time when you hated speaking into the radio," Damien remarked, eyes forward.

Louis kept his eyes forward too. "No one likes the sound of their own voice."

Damien grinned. "True. Did you guys get home alright last night?"

"Yeah," replied Louis. He suddenly found his courage and looked over at Damien. "Are we going to talk about what happened?"

"If you want." Damien weaved briskly though the dark backstreets of an industrial estate, not making any eye contact. "Was I out of order?"

Louis gritted his teeth, not really knowing how to answer. "Why did you do it?"

Damien gave an amused chuckle. "Because I find you attractive."

His bluntness was disarming. "I thought you were with Amy?"

"Things change."

Louis turned away and looked out of the window. The landscape was familiar now. They had arrived at Garnett Street via a different route. He turned back to Damien, annoyed. "What does that even mean? And why did you just leave like that?"

Damien pulled the car over and set the handbrake. He turned to Louis, resting his elbow on the top of his seat. His steely-blue eyes were softer somehow as he said, "Look, let's focus on finding your missing kid for now. Afterwards, we can go somewhere and talk properly."

He extended his arm and his fingers grazed the side of Louis' headrest, close to but not quite touching his face. Louis felt the hairs on the back of his neck stand straight up and the blood rush to his cheeks.

"Maybe you'll let me kiss you again?" Damien ventured with a playful smile. "Or we can just talk. Whatever you want."

With that, he started the car in motion again. Louis sat back in his seat, his heart racing as he processed what Damien had just said. Before he could finish his train of thought, he spotted a familiar blonde nest of peroxide curls bobbing up and down in the distance. "Quick! Pull over and speak to her."

Damien did as he was told. Louis jumped out of the car and spoke to the woman he'd given his Red Bull to the other night.

"Hello again, love," she said chirpily. There was a strong odour of alcohol on her breath tonight. "You lot are down here all the time lately. It's driving off all the punters. Looking for your little friend again?"

"Have you seen him?" Louis asked urgently.

"Last night," she nodded. "Stupid kid. He got into a car. I started this shite when I were fifteen. It's no life."

"Car details?" Damien leaned out of the window intently.

The woman beamed at him, evidently liking what she saw, but turned back to Louis and spoke to him. "Grey Volvo. Hang on."

She opened up her little black handbag and rummaged around, finally pulling out a notebook. She pointed to a registration number. "That's it. I always make a note of the dodgy punters. The ones that go for kids, I got no time for them. Dirty bastards."

She spat on the ground emphatically then reached into her bag again to avail herself of a compact vodka bottle.

Louis quickly scribbled down the registration in his own pocket notebook. Damien peered over and took the details as well. "Anything else you can tell me? What about the driver?"

As he was speaking to her, he heard Damien passing the vehicle details over the radio and asking the operator to perform a check on the Police National Computer for the registered keeper and insurance details.

"I didn't see him well. White bloke. That's about it. He spoke to the kid for a second then the kid got in on his own."

"What's your name?"

"Carla North," she replied. "Look me up if you need to, I'm not wanted."

"Get in!" Damien barked at Louis. Whilst they had been talking, the PNC check results had been passed by the operator.

Louis didn't hesitate. As he ran round to the passenger door, Damien illuminated the blue lights. Without waiting for Louis to fasten his seatbelt, Damien powered the car forward and activated the siren.

CHAPTER 13

The police car screamed through the streets, weaving like quicksilver round any obstacles without slowing. Louis was feeding information to the operator through the radio, allowing Damien to focus on the road.

They were moments away from Wycombe Crescent, a street in the affluent eastern suburbs of the city. This was the address to where the car that had picked up Connor was registered. The keeper was recorded as Bryan Hillesley, the operator advised. No warning markers. No relevant history. The house had been the location of a sudden death three years ago, an elderly lady with the same surname. The assumption was that Bryan had inherited the house.

Why the hell would Connor be there? Louis wondered. A flare of light from the street dazzled him momentarily. He spoke into his radio. "4029. Speed camera activation, Fraser Road."

It was good practice to let the control room know if any traffic cameras were triggered during a response run. Louis didn't need to see the speedometer to know that Damien was well over the speed limit. He had been on plenty of response runs with Luke before, but Damien was another class altogether. His eyes were focussed on the road, his head only moving to check for approaching traffic as they flew past junctions towards their destination. Man and machine had melded seamlessly. As much as Louis was focussed on the job ahead, he took a moment to acknowledge that his heart wasn't just racing because of the speed they were travelling.

Damien killed the blue lights as they turned into Wycombe Crescent. Louis sent the Code 6 signal, letting control know they were at the scene. Their body-cams activated automatically. Units were coming from across the city but they were the first here. They drew up outside a red-brick bungalow. The curtains in the front window were drawn but the lights were on.

As soon as the car halted, Louis took off up the tarmac driveway, passing the grey Volvo on his way. Damien was hot on his heels. Louis reached the side door and knocked hard.

"We haven't got a red key," Damien told him, referring to the heavy metal battering ram that would take most doors off their hinges.

Louis nodded and knocked again, harder this time. "Police!"

Damien ran round the corner to the back of the house. A second later, he shouted, "Louis! Hillesley's in there! He's run into the hallway!"

Louis didn't hesitate. He rammed the sole of his right boot into the door, just under the handle. It burst open and he charged in, yelling once more, "Police!"

He ran through a dark, narrow hallway into a bright, open-plan living room and dining room. The fug of fried food and stale body odour hung in the air. Hillesley stood with his back to the living room window, panting with fright in grey joggers and a white t-shirt. His arm raised like a tennis player about to serve. Louis saw the black iron poker in his hand.

Before he could react, Damien had darted past him, Taser raised. "Put it down!"

So fierce was Damien's voice that even Louis flinched. Hillesley was frozen on the spot, the colour drained from his face. Damien took his right leg back, bracing himself. "Put the poker down now!"

Louis saw a red dot appear on Hillesley's chest. The Taser was armed and ready to discharge if Damien moved his trigger-finger a touch more. Hillesley dropped the poker to the ground and lifted his hands in the air.

Damien barked instructions. "Turn around! Face the window. Hands in the air! Do it now!"

Hillesley complied without argument, moving as fast as his plump body would allow.

"Lie on your belly! Cross your ankles! Do it now!" Damien yelled. The purpose of getting him into this position wasn't to humiliate him. If he decided to stop complying, it would take him a split second longer to attack, giving Damien and Louis time to react. Damien nodded at Louis, signalling to move in. Louis drew his handcuffs and leapt forward, careful not to obstruct Damien's line of fire. He grabbed Hillesley's right wrist, applied one cuff then brought it behind his back and secured the left one in the other cuff. He checked them for tightness, ensuring there was enough room for blood to flow to his hands but not so much that he could slip them off.

Damien holstered his Taser and stepped forward. Together, they lifted Hillesley to his feet and patted him down, checking for anything that might help him escape or injure someone.

"Connor McAllen!" said Louis. "Where is he?"

Hillesley gasped wetly, snot running down his nose and onto his thick lips, but said nothing.

"Search the house," Damien said, taking a firm hold of Hillesley's left upper arm.

Louis dashed out of the living room and down the long, dark corridor. The next room on the right was the bathroom. Nothing. The main bedroom, decorated in sallow, flocked wallpaper was empty. The final door led to another bedroom.

"Connor!" Louis rushed to the double bed where Connor lay on his back, eyes closed. He was almost as pale as the cream floral duvet. Louis looked around. The extra lighting in the room was like an amateur film set. He spotted the expensive-looking computer equipment in the far corner of the room.

Louis didn't like the look of what he saw but the priority now was Connor. Louis shouted to Damien that he'd found Connor then yanked the pillow from behind his head. He lowered his ear to Connor's face and squeezed his eyes shut in relief when he felt Connor's breath tickle his cheek. Louis turned him onto his side in the recovery position then activated his radio. "4029. Expedite an ambulance to this address. Fourteen-year-old male, breathing but unconscious."

The operator confirmed an ambulance was on route. Louis knelt down and tapped repeatedly at Connor's cheek with his hand, calling his name. No response. He kept going, telling Connor to wake up. When that didn't work, he pinched Connor's earlobe hard between his thumb and forefinger. He saw Connor's face crease up and applied pressure again. Connor's eyelids fluttered open. His brilliant blue eyes were the most wonderful things Louis had seen all day.

"You're ok, Connor," he said, rubbing the boy's arm and shoulder. "Come on, wake up."

Louis was no expert but he knew this was more than just a sleepy teenager. He didn't smell alcohol. "Connor, have you taken anything?"

Connor blinked, looking confused. "Louis?"

"That's right," he replied, smiling. "You're safe. What have you taken?"

"Nothing," said Connor, closing his eyes again.

Louis pressed his hand to Connor's forehead. "No, mate, don't go back to sleep. Stay awake for me now, ok?"

Connor opened his eyes again and tried to sit up. Louis helped him. Connor looked around the room, squinting at the light. His gazed finally came to rest on his bare feet, which were stretched out in front of him. Connor frowned, "Louis?"

"Yeah?" Louis rubbed Connor's back, trying to keep him alert.

"He took my clothes off." Connor blinked hard thrust his chin out towards his feet. Louis followed his gaze but didn't see anything untoward, save for a healed scar on the arch of Connor's right foot.

"Just your socks, mate," said Louis. "Don't worry, I'll find them in a minute."

Connor shook his head, frustrated, then repeated emphatically, "He. Took. My. Clothes. Off."

Louis looked round the room again. The ring lights around the bed. The fancy computer equipment. An empty camera tripod. He suddenly felt very worried. "What's happened here, Connor?"

Connor's eyes flickered and he said again, "He took my clothes off."

Louis felt his jaw clench tightly. He propped Connor up against the headboard then marched back into the living room. Damien hadn't moved from the spot with Bryan Hillesley.

"Have you locked him up yet?" Louis asked. When Damien shook his head, Louis turned to Hillesley and said, "I'm arresting you on suspicion of kidnap and sexual activity with a child. You do not have to say anything, but it may harm your defence if you do not mention, when questioned, something which you later rely on in court. Anything you do say may be given in evidence. The necessity for your arrest is for a prompt, effective investigation and to protect a vulnerable child."

Louis caught a glimmer of pride in Damien's eyes and the hint of a smile. He quickly noted the time of arrest on the back of his hand then went back to the bedroom. As he stepped into the corridor, his radio chirped with a point-to-point call. "Go ahead."

"PC Mortimer, can you speak?" came a female voice with a strong northeastern accent. Louis told her to go ahead and she continued. "I'm DS Ryan, Operation Hollowpoint. Tell me what's going on there."

Louis had no idea who she was, or what Op Hollowpoint was for that matter, but updated her anyway.

"Ok," she said. "You've done a great job so far. Are you SOLO-trained?"

Sexual Offence Liaison Officers were specially-trained response officers dispatched to victims of rape and serious sexual assaults. Their role was to gather evidence of the assault sensitively and as early as possibly to prevent it from being lost.

"No, not yet," replied Louis. "I've done Early Evidence Kits before, though. Connor's really out of it. I'm not going to be able to complete an initial account pack with him just now."

"That's fine. If you feel confident to do it, get the EEK done as soon as you can then take him to Freedom House. Do you know where that is?"

Louis knew. Freedom House was a specialist centre where forensic medical examinations were carried out on victims of rape and sexual assault. It also had its own interview suite and video link room. He'd transported a couple of people there in the past.

"Sarge, I think we need to put a scene on at this house and get Digital Investigations down here to look at these computers." He explained his reasoning to DS Ryan.

"Spot on," she replied. "I'll get in touch with the shift commander to get some additional units down there. You just focus on the kid. I'm dispatching one of my cops to meet you at Freedom House. We'll give them the heads-up that you're on your way."

Louis acknowledged the message and ended the call. Two paramedics entered the room and greeted them both. Louis quickly relayed the circumstances to them and let them set to work checking Connor out. He seemed to be coming round a bit now. "Louis, is my mum here?"

"No, mate," he replied. "Just you and the guy who lives here."

Connor's despair was evident. "He said she'd be here."

"Your blood pressure's a little high, but ok," said the paramedic, unstrapping the cuff from Connor's arm. "Anything to eat or drink tonight?"

"Cheese on toast and some Pepsi," Connor murmured, looking around the room again as if taking it in for the first time.

"You're not in any trouble, lad," said the paramedic matter-of-factly, "But I need to know if you've had any drugs or alcohol."

Connor shook his head. "That's all I had, then I went to sleep. The next thing, Louis woke me up."

Now that he was more alert, Louis tried again. "Connor, why do you think he took off your clothes?"

Connor pointed at his bare feet. "I wouldn't have taken my socks off here. In case I needed to run."

Louis understood now. When his parents were at their worst, he had slept with his socks and school plimsolls on, ready to flee if his dad carried out his bellowed threats to burn the house down with them all inside.

The paramedic stood up and asked to speak to Louis in the hallway. Once out of Connor's earshot, he said, "I'm happy enough that he doesn't have to go to hospital. I think he's been given ketamine or similar to knock him out."

Louis replied, "I thought so too. I'm taking him to Freedom House."

The paramedic nodded and went back in to finish up. Louis heard voices in the kitchen and saw Noreen and Jack heading over to him. He smiled, grateful to see them.

"Louis, what can we do?" Noreen asked, returning a warm smile of her own.

Louis felt surprisingly focussed and calm. "There's an EEK in the boot, I'll need that. Grab our keys off Damien. And a Tyvek suit, if there's one. We're going to need to lock this house down as a scene, get the prisoner transported to custody and get Connor down to Freedom House."

"I'll get the circs off Damo then we'll book the prisoner in for you," Jack confirmed.

As they split back up, Louis relayed the plan over the radio to the operator, advising that the prisoner would need to be booked into a dry cell with no wash allowed until further notice. This was an accepted measure that prevented a suspect washing away delicate forensic evidence before the appropriate samples could be taken.

The paramedics bustled past, taking their kit with them and bidding goodnight. Louis waved them off. Damien popped his head round from the living room. "All ok?"

Louis nodded. "Have I forgotten anything?"

"You're doing just fine, mate."

Noreen returned with a small carboard box and a thin polythene bag containing the Tyvek suit. She followed Louis into the bedroom. Connor was sat with his legs hanging off the side of the bed. Louis knelt down in front of him and said, "We're going to take you to see a doctor and get checked out, buddy. If you're saying he's taken your clothes off, we need to find out what's happened. Is that ok?"

Connor nodded. "What if my mum turns up looking for me?"

"There's going to be some cops staying here to watch the place," he replied. "If she comes, they'll let me know. I need to take a couple of samples first, ok?"

Louis opened the white box that Noreen had brought. He slipped on the latex gloves from inside then drew out a sealed plastic tub of water. He handed it to Connor then drew out a screw-top beaker. "Ok, mate, when you're ready, open this water and swill it round your mouth. Count to thirty in your head then spit it into this beaker. Understand?"

Connor did as he was told. Once he spat out the water, Louis placed the sealed beaker in an evidence bag.

"Good lad. Do you think you can pee?"

"Fuck yes," Connor groaned, standing up. Louis and Noreen walked with him to the toilet. Louis handed him another beaker and explained what to do. Connor took it from him and closed the door. He reappeared a moment later with his sample. Louis repeated the same process of sealing it in an evidence bag and completing the details on the label.

Louis unwrapped the Tyvek suit and passed it to Connor to slip over himself. It was ridiculously big on him and Connor said as much. Louis made light of it, which made Connor grin. Louis knew there was potentially forensic evidence on Connor's clothes, but it would be better to seize them in the sterile environment of Freedom House; chances were that they would at least have some clothes for Connor to change into.

Noreen went into the living room to swap places with Damien. There were no issues with cross-contamination, Louis figured, because Connor had been in the house with Hillesley. When Damien joined them, his demeanour seemed more relaxed and friendly. He said to Connor, "Come on, mate. Let's get you on your way."

They walked down the driveway with him and helped him into the back of the car. Louis closed the door and looked around. Curtains along the street were already twitching at the sight of the police cars. A thought occurred to him and he pulled out his handheld terminal to make a phone call.

"Louis?" Aliyah's voice answered. "Is everything ok?"

"There isn't a simple answer to that," he replied mirthlessly then regaled the events to her.

When he had finished, she asked, "So, are they planning to video-interview him at Freedom House?"

Visually-recorded interviews, or VRIs as safeguarding professionals often referred to them, were a way of taking statements from children and vulnerable people. Instead of an officer writing down what had happened, a specially-trained detective would interview the person and the conversation was audio and visually-recorded. The recording could be played to the court at trial in lieu of a written statement.

"I'm not sure," replied Louis. "They're sending a detective down to meet me there."

"OK," replied Aliyah. "I'll come anyway. You'll need me there to consent to the medical examination as his corporate parent. If they want to interview him, I'll stay and be his interview supporter."

With all the arrangements agreed, Louis hung up and got in the car. Damien put it into gear and moved them off out of Wycombe Crescent in the direction of Freedom House.

CHAPTER 14

Freedom House was a relatively unassuming redbrick building tucked away on a semi-suburban street behind black iron fencing. To a passerby, it could easily have been mistaken for a doctor's surgery.

Damien pulled the car up to the electronic gate, pressed the buzzer and drove through when it opened. Louis glanced in the rearview mirror. Connor had sat quietly throughout the journey, gazing out of the window. Louis had left him to his thoughts until now. "Ready?"

Connor nodded and waited for Louis to open the door. Unsurprisingly, police vehicles had child-locks engaged. Damien told Louis he'd stay in the car and start writing up their report. Louis figured this sort of place wasn't Damien's milieu and let him be.

He and Connor walked to the front door and were greeted by a cheerful, middle-aged woman in scrubs named Gwen. She had a warm smile. Gwen steered Connor inside with a gentle hand on his shoulder. Aliyah was already in the building. Her brow furrowed when she saw him shuffle in wearing the oversized Tyvek suit. She came over and gave Connor a hug, evidently relieved to see him.

They were joined by the doctor, a slender woman with short white hair, who introduced herself as Maria. She spoke directly to Connor, making sure he was happy for her to examine him and talking him through what would happen.

After they had finished talking, she took Louis and Aliyah into an office whilst Gwen led Connor to the examination room. They sat down in some easy chairs and Maria consulted her notes. "It's been quite a time for this young man, hasn't it?"

Just then, the door opened and the receptionist admitted a tall Asian woman. Louis spotted her police warrant card, which dangled from the lanyard around her neck.

"So sorry I'm late," she said, sitting down and pulling a blue A4 notebook from her handbag. "I'm DC Sabina Hussein."

Louis studied her. She was stunning. Dark brown skin, wavy black hair cut short enough to frame her sharp cheekbones and the most striking pair of green eyes he had ever seen. She wore a light green blazer over a white blouse and black jeans. Louis noticed Aliyah staring enviously at her sleek black ankle boots.

"Not at all, DC Hussein, we were just starting," said Maria. She reeled off the details she had been given, checking for accuracy. Aliyah and Sabina listened intently as Louis confirmed the doctor's notes.

"Great that you've done a urine sample as part of the EEK," she said. "If he can provide another whilst he's here, I'll test it for the presence of ketamine. It won't be reliable enough to be used in court, so you'll need to submit the sample for a proper forensic analysis, but at least you'll have an indication. And he hasn't fully disclosed sexual assault?"

"No," replied Louis. "He's really clear, though, that the suspect took his clothes off whilst he was unconscious. Connor says he would never have taken his socks off to go to sleep in a stranger's house but when he woke up, he was barefoot."

"Interesting," murmured Maria. "What I propose, in that case, is just a cursory anogenital examination unless anything new comes to light as we proceed. Of course, I'll complete a full top-to-toe injury check of his body. We'll screen for sexually-transmitted infections too, but we'll need him to come back in six weeks for follow-ups."

"I'll take care of that," said Aliyah.

"We'll need his clothing," Sabina said.

Maria nodded. "PC Mortimer had the bright idea of bringing him to us in a Tyvek suit. We'll bag everything up for you as we go. Will you be carrying out the VRI here?"

Sabina nodded. "If he's willing. Let's see how he's doing after the examination. Louis, will you be able to do notes for me?"

"Marvellous," said Maria, standing up. "Right, let's not keep Connor waiting any longer. DC Hussein, I believe you've been here before? Do show your colleagues around and help yourselves to drinks and food in the kitchen."

They parted ways in the corridor. Louis and Aliyah followed Sabina to a kitchen with a round table in the middle. She invited them to sit whilst she made a round of hot drinks. When she brought them over and sat down herself, she said, "Well, with any luck, we'll be able to get him interviewed tonight and then he can focus on recovering. You've done a great job, Louis. My sergeant was well impressed."

Louis blushed. "Thanks, I hope so. Did they get the suspect to custody ok?"

"Yes," replied Sabina. "They've got an interview team with him now taking his first account. Good call on his computers, by the way. Digital Investigation Team triaged them in situ and they're full of indecent images of children."

"Has he taken any of Connor," Aliyah asked, her face furrowed with concern.

"Too soon to tell," Sabina replied. "Rest assured, though, we'll nail him to the wall."

Louis liked her. She spoke with a reassuring confidence, exuding a sense of kindness. "I've never done notes for a VRI before."

"It's easy," Sabina said, smiling. "Don't worry about doing them verbatim. Just listen to what's being said and think about what we need to know. When I've got Connor's account, I'll come out to check with you. I'll need you to tell me if I've missed anything, no matter how small."

Louis nodded. They sipped their drinks silently and waited.

* * * * *

Two hours later, the receptionist asked them to join Maria in the office again so she could share her findings.

"Let me start with the good news," she said, taking a sip of water. "There are no immediate indicators of penetrative sexual abuse."

Louis heard Aliyah utter a sigh of relief. He almost reached over to squeeze her hand, letting her know she wasn't the only one having that feeling. The irony wasn't lost on him, the two of them sat there like fraught parents.

Maria continued, "I have, however, taken swabs from his mouth, penis and anus for reasons I'll explain in a moment. I recommend that you have them tested by the lab for evidence of suspect DNA. I considered taking rectal swabs, but I felt that would be disproportionate given that Connor hasn't disclosed penetrative abuse and there were no outward signs of anal trauma. I'll document the rationale for my decision fully in my report. We tested a fresh urine sample and there was evidence of ketamine in it, so we need to be alert to the possibility that Connor may not be aware of everything that has happened to him."

"What do you think has happened, doctor?" Sabina asked, her pen poised over her open notebook.

"Connor repeated his observation regarding his socks," replied Maria. She smiled. "He's a very astute young man. As part of the injury check, I examined his body under alternative light sources. Aside from the usual lumps and bumps you would expect for an active teenager, I found evidence of staining on his abdomen."

Sabina stopped writing and looked up. "Staining?"

"Yes, consistent with ejaculation."

Louis didn't want to say it so was relieved when Sabina asked the question. "As you say, he's a teenage boy. Surely it could just be..."

"I'd considered that possibility," Maria replied without a hint of condescension. She drew her finger up from her navel towards her breastbone. "I'd expect staining caused through masturbation to travel vertically. The pattern I've found is more consistent with someone kneeling beside Connor whilst he has been laid on his back and ejaculating across him. The semen appears to have been wiped, but not with any sort of soap. Dry tissue paper, more than likely. I've taken swabs from the semen."

Aliyah spoke up next. "What about the ketamine in his system?

155

Will he need more treatment?"

"Ketamine is actually a relatively safe drug for children, even those with asthma," said Maria. "Obviously, I mean that in the context of it being given in a medical setting. It doesn't appear that Connor has been given much, just enough to sedate him for a while. He will recover just fine without any lasting damage. I'm more concerned that he's quite dehydrated. I've contacted Paediatrics at Valley View General and they'll admit him for overnight observation."

Everyone nodded in agreement.

"Marvellous," said Maria, standing up. "Connor's gone for a shower and to change into some fresh clothes. Gwen will sign over the clothing he was wearing when he came here. It's all bagged and tagged. He seems to be managing ok so I suspect he'll be willing to provide his VRI tonight.

* * * * *

Gwen brought Connor into the waiting room of the VRI suite, where Louis, Aliyah and Sabina were sat in coarse, dark-blue armchairs. Louis looked over at Connor and smiled encouragingly. His blond curls were damp from the shower but still springy. He was wearing a plain black t-shirt and grey joggers. The only things of his own were his black trainers. Maria had asked whether they required seizing as evidence and Sabina had decided not – there would unlikely be any forensic benefit from examining them. Louis felt a pang of worry as Connor stepped more into the light. He looked paler than usual and very tired.

Connor sat down in the free armchair and Gwen left the room. Louis handed Connor a pre-packaged chicken sandwich he'd found in the kitchen and then introduced him to Sabina. Connor wolfed it down as Sabina explained the VRI process.

"It's Louis' first time as well, so I need to show him how everything works," said Sabina. "Do you want to come with us?"

Connor nodded and followed them through the door on the left. Inside was a desk, a monitor, a control console and a large black box that Louis recognised as a recording device; they had the same type in the custody interview rooms.

"So, this is where you and Aliyah will sit," Sabina said. "Louis, you just need to make sure that the cameras are covering Connor and that the sound is coming through ok. You switch the recorder on and off like you would do with the ones in custody."

Louis liked what Sabina was doing. Giving Connor a bit of control, not patronising him but still letting him know what was going to happen. "Connor, I hope you don't find mind if Aliyah sits in here? It saves her having to ask you the same questions and you having to go through everything again. Plus, she knows you a lot better than I do, so if she sees you getting tired or if I'm not asking you things in the best way, she'll be able to tell me."

"Yeah, it's ok," murmured Connor. "You better let Louis work the cameras though, she's shit with technology."

Aliyah's mouth went wide with faux outrage and she clipped him gently around the back of his head.

"Duly noted, my friend," laughed Sabina. "Louis' going to stay in here to make sure all the equipment works ok, and to make sure I don't forget to ask you anything. Once we've done talking, I'll nip through to check with him."

Sabina led them back through into the waiting room then into the door on the right. This door was decidedly heavier. The room was sparse, just two armchairs opposite each other and a low round table with some pens and blank paper between them. Something about the room made Louis' ears feel strange.

"That's just the soundproofing," Sabina told them. "Once the door's shut, no one outside of this room and the monitor room will be able to hear what's being said."

She patted the armchair at the far corner of the room. "This is where you'll sit, Connor. Give it a go?"

Connor dropped heavily into it and stretched his legs out in front of him. "Where are the cameras."

Sabina knelt down beside him and pointed up to two white domes, one in the upper left-hand corner of the room and the other behind her chair. "Right there. And those little black things that look like speakers on the wall, they're the microphones."

Connor got back up to examine them more closely. As he did, Sabina turned to face Louis and asked, "So, do you understand everything? Ready to go?"

Louis nodded. "I am if Connor is."

Connor gave a thumbs up. Aliyah came over and gave him a hug. He chided her for being soft but didn't push her away. Louis watched them, pleased that Aliyah was so natural and warm towards him. He couldn't imagine his social workers, or even his foster carers, offering physical affection. As much as he would have happily given Connor a hug himself, he limited himself to a squeeze of Connor's shoulder. "Good luck, buddy."

They left Connor and Sabina in the room to get settled. In the monitor room, Louis adjusted the cameras for the best view of Connor. The main screen displayed the feed from the camera behind Sabina's chair, which focussed in on Connor's face. The smaller inset of the second camera showed the whole room, presumably to demonstrate to the court that no one else was in the room influencing the interview. Sabina signalled that she was ready and Louis started the recording.

Louis watched and listened intently as Sabina introduced the interview, gave her formal title, the date and time. She ran through the ground-rules of the interview with Connor, reassuring him that all he needed to do was tell her what he knew; it was fine if there was something he didn't remember or wasn't sure about. She followed with a basic scenario that was meant to demonstrate to the court that he knew the difference between the truth and a lie, and the potential consequences of telling a lie. Then it was over to Connor.

As he told Sabina what had happened, everything started to fall into place for Louis. Hillesley had been manipulating Connor by pretending to be his mum, encouraging him to run away in order to try and find her. Louis frowned and wrote in his notes, "How did he get Connor's number?"

Connor recounted Hillesley bringing him to his house, telling him that Emma would be there waiting. She had wanted to come with him to pick Connor up but she was feeling rough. Connor looked away from the camera as he told Sabina that Emma was a drug user, so sometimes she felt too ill to even get up.

Louis and Aliyah glanced at each other, their hearts silently breaking for him.

Connor went on to say that he had been worried when they'd got to Hillesley's house and Emma wasn't there. He'd tried to reassure himself that maybe she'd had to go out to pick up her methadone or something. There were times when the doctor wouldn't allow her to have her dose unless she went to the chemist and took it in front of the pharmacist.

Hillesley had been calm and welcoming. He'd let Connor sit in the living room and watch whatever he wanted on Netflix whilst he went into the office in his bedroom to carry on working. Eventually, Hillesley had offered to make him a snack and a drink. He'd offered him beer and spirits but Connor had refused them in favour of a soft drink. Hillesley had returned with cheese on toast and a glass of Pepsi.

Louis scribbled on his notes, "Description of glass."

If Luke were here, he'd have bet Louis a Snickers Bar that's how Hillesley administered the ketamine.

Connor remembered suddenly feeling very sleepy and Hillesley taking him to the bedroom to lie down. That was the last thing he recalled before he woke up to Louis shaking him and pinching his ear. Sabina deliberately didn't ask him about any sexual activity because Connor hadn't introduced it; this stage of the interview was led by him. However, Connor demonstrated the astuteness that Maria had remarked on. "I don't remember anything sexual happening but I would never have let him."

Sabina shifted seamlessly into the second phase of the interview where she asked questions to probe what Connor had said and clarify details. She asked him for a description of the glass and where he last saw it. Louis anticipated she would relay that detail to the Crime Scene Investigators so that they could photograph the glass in situ and seize it for forensic testing.

Sabina asked Connor whether he used any illicit substances with Hillesley or in general, to which he said no on both counts. She then asked him to clarify his comment about sexual activity.

Connor looked directly at the camera, his blue eyes seemingly boring into Louis' soul. "How I grew up, you've got to be ready to run. I would *never* have taken my socks off in that bastard's house. Maybe my trainers, but no way my socks too. I always need to be ready to go."

Louis looked over at Aliyah, who was shaking her head quietly. She wiped a tear from her cheek then went back to her notes.

Sabina rounded up her questions then excused herself from the interview room to join Louis and Aliyah. "He's done really well. Anything I've missed?"

Louis passed on his observation about how Hillesley had gotten Connor's number.

"Brilliant!" she beamed and headed back into the interview room. When she was seated, she said to Connor, "Louis raised a question when I checked in with him."

"Big surprise," Connor retorted with a smile. "Man never shuts up with the questions."

He listened to Sabina's question then shrugged. He had no idea how Hillesley had gotten his number. It wasn't something he shared widely, even with other young people he knew. He certainly hadn't given it over any chat rooms or social media. If anything, he had given it to more professionals because they all wanted to contact him for whatever reason.

Louis frowned, pondering that comment. He heard Sabina confirm that the interview was over and deactivated the recorder.

They reconvened in the waiting room to discuss next steps. Connor was none too happy when he found out he was going to hospital for the night.

"It's just a precaution," said Aliyah. "I'll take you there so Sabina and Louis can get on with what they need to do. If the hospital gives you the all-clear in the morning, I'll come get you and bring you home."

Connor exhaled wearily. "Fine. Elliott's probably going to want me to catch up on a fuck-ton of school work now. Might as well do it in the comfort of my own children's home. Alright then, Big Al, let's go. I'll let you buy me a McFlurry on the way."

"It would be my honour, Mr McAllen," replied Aliyah drily, smiling.

They bade farewell to Gwen and the receptionist then stepped out into the car park. Sabina excused herself to make a call to her boss. Aliyah had parked next to the police car so they walked in that direction.

Connor went up to the driver's side of the police car and tapped on the window. Damien wound it down and popped his head out. "All done, mate?"

Connor nodded. "Yeah. I wanted you to meet Big Al, my social worker. Big Al, this is Lurch. He looks like he enjoys a meal out at Nando's. Maybe you should offer to take him one night?"

Louis put his hand to his mouth, trying not to crease up laughing at Aliyah's mortified expression. He caught Damien's perplexed grin in his direction and smiled back.

Aliyah ushered Connor into her car, keen to avoid any further humiliation. She thanked Louis for his help and said she'd call him to confirm when Connor was admitted. Louis watched them drive off then saw Sabina walking over to join him. "Just been updating my boss. The DCI's asked if you can call up to see her before you book off. Shall we go?"

Louis frowned but agreed all the same, not that he had a choice. The mental box of Simon-isms sprung open once more and poured forth all the things he had done wrong with this job, which the DCI would no doubt want to point out to him. He braced himself for the news that he'd probably done something so dumb it would crash the entire job. He got into the car with Damien and they headed back to Weaver's Yard with Sabina in tow.

CHAPTER 15

Sabina led Louis and Damien into a small office, partitioned off from the main open-plan office on Weaver's Yard Police Station's fifth floor. When they had walked through the main doors, Louis had noted that the sign said Op Hollowpoint. Apparently, Sabina's team was separate to the main Child Protection Team.

Sat behind the desk was an athletic-looking black woman in a navy-blue suit. Her striking brown eyes were made all the more so by the fact that her head was shaved.

"Ah, hello!" she exclaimed, jumping up from her desk and joining them on the other side. She wasn't particularly tall, but she had big energy. "DCI Karen Lucas."

"Ma'am," Louis and Damien replied in unison.

She looked Damien up and down. "Blimey, you're tall. Would you mind giving Sabina a hand booking on her exhibits whilst I speak to your colleague here?"

Damien let himself be led out of the office by Sabina. DCI Lucas returned to her seat and tented her hands. Louis remained standing, unsure whether to take a seat without being bidden. At this point, he still had no idea of how much trouble he was in.

"I reviewed the body-cam footage of you going in to get Connor,"

Lucas said finally. Her voice was stern. "Just what exactly was your rationale for that, PC Mortimer?"

Louis swallowed hard. "All the information I had suggested that there was a child at risk in there, Ma'am."

"But Hillesley has no history of sexual offences, no warning markers. How can you justify that?"

"Ma'am, he picked up the boy from the city's red-light area. That led me to believe there might be a sexual risk."

Lucas' face hardened. "And precisely what legal enactment did you feel gave you the power to just kick someone's door in like that?"

"PACE, section seventeen. I had reasonable grounds to suspect life and limb was at stake," replied Louis, clenching his jaw. Why was she grilling him like this? Was there some problem with his decision to go in?

"Take a seat, PC Mortimer," said Lucas finally.

He did as he was told and waited for whatever was about to be unleashed.

"Bloody. Good. Work." Each word was punctuated with a slap of her hand on the desk. "You've saved that young man from some really serious harm and given us a rock-solid case to boot."

Louis blinked. "Thank you, Ma'am."

Lucas rested back in her chair. "You're only just signed off, correct? Have you heard of Hollowpoint before?"

Stumbling over his words a little, Louis confirmed that he had just been signed off but had never heard of Hollowpoint.

"We're the force's response to children that are being sexually-exploited. You'll no doubt have seen in the media that these non-recent cases are now coming to light and are being successfully prosecuted. Well, Hollowpoint is working with current cases."

Louis nodded, unsure of what this all had to do with him.

"Annie Porter's husband tutored you, right?"

"Yes, Ma'am."

"Annie speaks highly of you, as does Luke."

Louis took the compliment but felt his face get hot all the same.

"I believe both of them have suggested that you consider moving into this line of work?"

"Yes, but..." Louis started.

Lucas wasn't interested in him finishing that sentence. "I'm impressed with the work you've done on this case, Louis. I'd like to offer you a place on Hollowpoint. It would be a six-month attachment to begin with, a try-before-you-buy arrangement. In any event, you've developed an excellent working relationship with Connor and I'd like to make sure we keep him on board, so it makes sense for you to stay involved with him."

Louis finally managed to gather himself. "I appreciate the offer, Ma'am. Could I have some time to think about it?"

"Of course," she replied. "But, consider this. At your level of service, you've built rapport with a vulnerable child and seen him through some traumatic but necessary investigative processes. You've apprehended the perpetrator and created a handover package to my unit that has been so meticulously constructed, I nearly wept with joy. Even the points you've raised with Sabina for the VRI tell me that you have a talent for this kind of work. With no disrespect to your friend next door, you'd be wasted in patrol."

It was like a repeat of his conversation with Luke. He nodded pensively.

"Anyway, I'll let you go for now," she said. "Have a think over your rest days and let me know when you get back on shift. If you're willing to join us, I'll make the arrangements with Chief Inspector Horton."

Louis thanked her and stood up. Before he left, he asked, "Would it be ok if I visited Connor in hospital?"

Lucas smiled and nodded. "I think he'd appreciate that, and so would I. However, we need to ensure that our contact with him is properly recorded. Whenever you go, make a note of the time, date, and duration of your visits along with any discussions you have. E-mail them to Sabina and to DS Ryan."

With that, she turned back to her computer screen and Louis took that as his dismissal.

He went into the main office to collect Damien, who was sat with Sabina.

"Fat lot of fucking help this one's been!" she exclaimed when Louis came over.

Damien smiled innocently. "What can I say? Booking on property isn't my strong point."

Sabina dismissed him with a playful wave and thanked Louis again for his help. Once they were out of the office, they walked to the lift and summoned it.

"So," Damien said, "What did the boss want?"

"I thought she was going to bollock me," replied Louis. "She's offered me a job on her operation."

"You should take it," Damien said. "It would suit you."

The lift arrived and they stepped in. As soon as the door closed, Damien wrapped his arms around Louis and kissed him. Louis was caught off guard but responded all the same, experiencing the same electricity rush through his body as he'd felt the other night.

"I've wanted to do that all night," said Damien, finally releasing him. "Do you still want to go somewhere and talk?"

"I have to go home and feed my cat," Louis murmured, savouring the taste of Damien on his lips. He mentally kicked himself for both sounding like a pathetic spinster and like he was inviting Damien home.

"Sounds like a plan," said Damien. "I'll stop off and get us something to eat."

The lift arrived on the basement floor and the doors opened. Louis followed Damien out into the car park and set off home. Throughout the journey, he watched Damien's red Mercedes AMG-A35 following him. There was part of Louis that didn't want this. He was still sleep-deprived from his night out and then the intense shift that he had just gone through. It didn't reassure him that he would make good decisions. On the other hand, he desperately wanted to see where this thing with Damien was leading.

* * * * *

Half an hour later, Louis opened his door to Damien, who was carrying a black hold-all in one hand and a white plastic bag in the other.

Louis stood aside and admitted him. Damien's large frame practically filled the hallway. He handed Louis the food, a curry from the local Punjabi restaurant judging by the aroma, and asked if he could freshen up.

Louis pointed him upstairs then took the food into the kitchen to dish out. He'd landed home, thrown off his work clothes in favour of some grey joggers and a blue t-shirt then splashed his face with cold water to try and revitalise himself.

As he split the pilau rice, a chicken curry that looked to be loaded with green chillies and garlic naan across two bowls, the surrealness of the situation hit him. This time last week, he could have counted on one hand the number of meaningful conversations he and Damien had had. They'd never even shared a packet of crisps, let alone a meal.

And now this, Louis frowned as Damien padded into kitchen. He'd changed into a pair of black tapered joggers and a frayed grey Guns 'n' Roses t-shirt. He smelt freshly of aftershave. He joined Louis at the breakfast bar and they started eating. Damien apologised in advance if the curry was too spicy. Not a problem for someone whose Mauritian father insisted on green chillies in everything, Louis reassured him. Their meal passed with light conversation, neither of them venturing into the territory that really needed to be spoken about.

Damien finally took them there. "So, last night then?"

Louis wasn't sure where to start. Too many questions buzzed about his head. "This just all feels so…. sudden. Two days ago, you were outside The Winston kissing a girl, next you're here with me."

Damien dropped his eyes and chuckled. "Yeah, it sounds bad

when you say it like that. Amy and I aren't seeing each other anymore, if that's what you're worried about? For the record, I went straight home after leaving you and I didn't have any company when I got there."

"I don't know what I'm worried about," Louis said, his jaw tensing in frustration. It made him feel a little better to know that Damien hadn't jumped straight into Amy's bed after kissing him. He got up and stacked their empty bowls into the dishwasher. "I just.....I don't know what this is? I don't need any headfucks right now. And I don't want to be used to work out whether or not you like guys as well as girls."

Louis leaned up against the worktop, hands gripping the edge to hold himself steady. The idea that he had been caught up in what could just be an experiment for Damien wasn't a pleasant one.

"It's true, this is all new to me," said Damien. He looked away, a shyness seemingly taking hold of him. "I've been thinking about you a lot. For a long time, in fact. I just wasn't brave enough to tell you. But when I saw you dancing with that guy last night, it made me realise I had to do something or I'd lose you."

He stood up and came over, sliding his arms between Louis' and resting his hands on the worktop so he could move in close. The energy between them was almost tangible. "I promise you, Louis, this isn't just something I'm trying on."

His words hung between them for a moment. Louis studied his earnest expression, trying to make a decision but totally distracted by Damien's closeness.

Finally, Damien sighed. "Look, I don't want to make your life complicated. If this is too much for you right now, I'll go."

Fuck. Louis felt frozen to the spot. The box of Simon-isms was slowly creaking open again. The complications of a relationship with a work colleague started to overwhelm him. Things wouldn't have been anywhere near as tricky with geeky Sam from Mama Kofi's.

"Do you want me to go?" Damien asked, bringing Louis back to the moment.

Louis slipped his arms around Damien's waist and interlocked his fingers at the small of his back. "No."

Damien's smile was pure happiness. Louis relaxed as Damien pulled him in closer and kissed him, a sense of relief washing over him like a wave.

* * * * *

Blessing Adebayo parked his security van in front of Low Dean Mills and got out, pulling on his uniform jacket. He shivered, once again pining for the heat and humidity of Lagos. After checking the charge on his radio, he approached the gates and undid the padlock so he could enter. Not that the padlock or the chain-link fencing surrounding the derelict sprawl of stone buildings, stained brown over time, stopped people getting in.

He hated coming here, so close to the area where women drifted up and down the streets all night, barely dressed and looking for business. Every so often, they would approach him and ask, even if he was in his work van. Blessing always refused, saying a quiet prayer for them. To be so desperate to resort to such things, it was heartbreaking. As he wandered up to the front entrance of the mill, he ruminated on the men that cruised back and forth through the darkened streets. Didn't they have wives and children to be spending time with? He thought of his own wife, at home now with their infant son.

Blessing unlocked the door and went inside, flicking on his torch. There were no lights to speak of in here. The air was dank. He listened to the steady drip-drip of the water leaking into the cavernous room. The floors had developed holes over time so it was possible in some spots to look up and see right through to the mill's roof. Blessing moved round slowly, deliberately making as much noise as possible. Just occasionally, a homeless person or drug addict would find their way in to get out of the cold and the rain. They rarely stayed long, knowing that security patrolled the mills.

Blessing flashed his torch to the right swiftly, hearing a rustle and seeing a shadow dart along the wall. Nothing. The other occupational hazard was foxes. Strange, eerie creatures that had a way of making Blessing feel like they were staring into his soul with their yellow eyes. He had screamed and ran the first time he saw one, afraid it would maul him. Over time, he became braver and learned that they tended to scarper at the sight of humans. All the same, he wasn't sure whether he preferred to come across a drug addict or a fox.

He turned his gaze and the torch beam back in front of him and continued stepping gingerly across the worn stone floor. Old rusty barrels were dotted around. Weeds and moss were abundant, particularly in the areas where water had leaked in. He kicked an empty beer can out from his path, sweeping his torch left to right as he walked.

Blessing halted in his tracks. He swung the torch towards a corner at the back of the vast room. He could have sworn....

"Hello?" he called out, stepping forward cautiously.

In the gloom, he saw an old green couch against the wall. That was nothing new. Someone had managed to move it in to sleep on.

The building management company couldn't be bothered to move it back out, preferring for the elements to rot it away slowly.

Someone was sat on it, looking at him. He squinted, making out blonde curly hair.

He started walking forward with more speed, trying to sound braver than he actually felt. "You are not allowed in here!"

The person, definitely a person, didn't move or respond.

Blessing reached the couch and shone the torch in their face. "Hey!"

Dead eyes stared back at him, the mouth hanging open languidly.

"Oh my god," he whispered, grasping the torch for dear life. He backed off, unable to break his gaze away from the lifeless blue eyes that studied him. He fumbled for his radio. "I need help now!"

CHAPTER 16

Louis was awoken by Gonzo's nose nudging at his forehead. His loud purring sounded almost inquisitive. Louis was laid on his side, cheek deeply embedded in the pillow. It took him a moment longer to remember that he wasn't alone. Damien's arm was draped over his waist. It was still early, half-seven by his phone's clock. He smiled to himself and snuggled back against Damien, who responded by pulling him in tighter.

They had stayed up talking a while longer before they succumbed to tiredness. Louis had resisted the urge to make things physical, choosing instead to savour the intimacy of just being close. Damien had seemed more than happy with that but nevertheless had taken every opportunity he could to kiss and cuddle. Louis' smile widened when he remembered Damien recounting in the dark how he'd fallen for him on Louis' first day. The attraction had only grown stronger the more they worked together. He'd confessed to being a little jealous that Luke had gotten to tutor Louis but had accepted that was probably for the best, given his feelings. Louis had tried to probe Damien's previous history with other men but had quickly sensed from Damien's closed reactions that this was a topic better left for another day. From what he could gather, this was uncharted territory for Damien.

Gonzo was becoming more strident in his investigations, clearly put out by another human taking up his space. Louis reached over and petted his head, which seemed to assuage him a little. He smiled as he felt Damien's lips brush against the side of his neck. "Hello."

Damien didn't reply immediately, continuing to kiss and nuzzle Louis' neck. "Hello. I guess he's feeling a little territorial?"

"Maybe a little. Wanting his breakfast, more likely," replied Louis, turning over. He slipped his arm around Damien's waist and kissed him. "Do you want something?"

"Whatever you're having." He gave Louis' bum a playful squeeze. "I suppose I should get going soon, let you get on with your day?"

Louis would have quite happily spent his day wrapped up like this in Damien's arms. "No rush."

He traced his fingers along the top of Damien's shoulder idly, following the swirls and pictures of his tattoos down towards his upper-right chest. When Damien had stripped off to his underwear to get into bed, Louis had had to dig deep to maintain his self-control. The work in the gym was definitely evident. He closed his eyes and murmured, "This is nice."

The spell was promptly broken by the insistent buzzing of his phone from the bedside table. Groaning, Louis unravelled himself from Damien and took the call.

"Louis?" A female voice. "Karen Lucas. Can you speak?"

Asking 'Can you speak' was a habit that every cop seemed to have, borne perhaps from making sure someone wasn't in the middle of wrestling a suspect into handcuffs as you point-to-pointed them. "Morning Ma'am. Yes, go ahead."

Louis sat up and swung his legs out of the bed. Damien got up and padded out of the bedroom to the bathroom.

"I'm sorry to call you on your rest day, but I thought you'd want to know."

Louis wondered whether she was ringing to give him an update on Hillesley, although he wouldn't have expected it from a boss of her rank.

"We charged Hillesley this morning," she said. "Between Connor's VRI, the forensic evidence and what we've found so far on his computers, he had no chance. CPS came back with a raft of charges for him. Make no mistake, he'll get a significant custodial sentence."

"That's great," replied Louis. "I really appreciate the update. Does Connor know?"

"Not yet," replied Karen. There was something in her voice that made Louis nervous. "There's some worrying news about the footage we found on Hillesley's mobile."

He braced himself for the other shoe to drop.

"Louis, there was someone else there."

He pressed his hand to his mouth. He'd never searched the bungalow properly. He'd never even asked Hillesley if there was anyone else in the house. Someone could have been hidden, waiting for a chance to destroy evidence as soon as the police locked the place down and left to stand guard outside. "I can't believe I missed it."

Karen didn't seem to understand what he was talking about and continued. "When we reviewed the mobile footage, we have Hillesley in the bedroom with Connor. He's seen taking Connor's clothes off, touching him and masturbating over him, but there's someone else talking to him and telling him what to do. Whoever it is, they stay out of shot. We think it's a male voice but we're not a hundred percent. Whoever it is doesn't speak long or loudly enough for us to be sure. We can't even pinpoint whether it's a local accent or from further afield. For reasons known only to himself, Hillesley is refusing to disclose who his accomplice is."

Louis shuddered. What had happened to Connor was horrendous enough, but it was even more chilling to think that someone had stood in the room giving directions.

"That's awful. Is there anything I can do?"

"Yes, there is," Karen replied, her voice becoming more tense. "Unfortunately, the bad news doesn't end there. Louis, I need you to understand that there's no obligation on you to do this. You are entirely in your rights to say no and get on with the remainder of your rest days."

"I'll do anything I can, Ma'am," said Louis, steeling himself.

No amount of steel could prepare him for what Karen told him next.

* * * * *

Louis strode through the hospital corridor in a daze. He was sure his pace was normal but it felt like slow motion. Maybe it was wishful thinking, anything to delay the awful task ahead of him. Aliyah was keeping in step to his right, her expression grave.

The door in front of them was opened by a nurse, Maggie, who was in charge. She had been waiting for them. After ushering them into a quiet room, she left them alone.

Louis sat back in one of the beige easy-chairs. Dressed in dark blue jeans and a baggy black jumper, he almost felt naked without his uniform; as if the layers of Kevlar might protect his heart from more than physical attack. He used his thumb and forefinger to rub his eyes. It was incomprehensible that he could have been so happy not two hours ago, intertwined with Damien, only to be brought now to the harshest extreme of life's spectrum.

Aliyah was silent, her gaze faraway. Louis wanted to say something, do something to offer some comfort; but he knew there wasn't any comfort to be had in the face of such sheer cruelty.

They both snapped back into the room as the door swung open. Maggie held it open and Connor breezed in. He was wearing the black T-shirt and grey joggers from Freedom House.

"S'up, peeps?" he said, plonking himself down in the chair beside Louis. "Am I getting a police escort home?"

Louis caught Aliyah's desperate glance. She couldn't do it.

Louis got up from his chair and knelt down next to Connor's. There was no easy way to say it, so he just said it. "They've found your mum. I'm so sorry, Connor, she's dead."

Connor blinked, barely moving a muscle. For a second, Louis thought he hadn't heard him. Then it came. A quake rippled from Connor's shoulders upwards to his face, his eyes welling up and his lips trembling.

An inhuman wail burst forth from Connor's mouth, somewhere between a scream and a roar, that clawed horribly at Louis' soul. He reacted just in time to catch Connor as he lurched forward out of his chair. Connor clung to Louis neck and sobbed hard into his shoulder. Louis held him tight, his own eyes beginning to tear up.

Aliyah was suddenly on her knees with them, her arms around

both Louis and Connor as she wept along with them.

* * * * *

"I'll get us some coffee," Aliyah said, standing up. Her voice was hoarse. "Do you want something to eat?"

From his seat next to Connor's bed, Louis shook his head. It was lunchtime now but he couldn't stomach anything. Maggie had moved Connor into a private room. When he had finally worn himself out crying, Connor had gone so limp that Louis had had to carry him back to the ward. He had laid on the bed in a foetal position, weeping softly until he dropped off into an exhausted sleep.

Louis felt heavy, like someone had poured lead into his lungs. Connor looked so fragile. How the hell could anyone take this much trauma and make it through? Aliyah touched his shoulder as she left and he squeezed her hand. Anyone looking in would have thought they were some strange little blended family.

His phone buzzed and he pulled it out. Damien's text was simply a heart emoji followed by a hugging one. Louis smiled. Damien had come back into the bedroom to find Louis sitting on the bed, stone-still and pale. He'd offered to come to the hospital too but Louis told him no. The fact that Damien had offered, though, meant a lot.

"Louis?"

He turned towards the doorway and saw Elliott standing there, a worried look on his face. Louis got up and went to the door. Elliott shook his hand then stepped back, allowing Louis to close the door so they could speak outside without waking Connor up.

"Aliyah called me," said Elliott. He looked exhausted, dark circles under his eyes. "How's Connor?"

"Not good," replied Louis. "He finally dropped off half an hour ago."

"Do we know how Emma died?"

Louis nodded. "The working theory is a drug overdose. She was found in Low Dean Mills just off Garnett Street. It looks like she'd taken some heroin that was cut with fentanyl."

Elliott frowned. "Fentanyl?"

"It's a synthetic opioid. It's a lot more potent than heroin, even for hardcore users. Tiny amounts can cause a fatal overdose. A briefing went out about it a while ago. Apparently, it's making its way up north."

"That poor woman," murmured Elliott, shaking his head sadly.

"Let's go back in," said Louis. "Connor will be glad to see you."

They moved quietly back into the room and Elliott drew up a chair next to Louis'. It felt like an age since Louis had seen him, the last time being in the carvery with his girlfriend. Despite them talking in hushed voices, Connor opened his eyes and sat up.

"Hey, buddy," Elliott said warmly, standing up and drawing him into a brief hug. "I'm so, so sorry."

Connor was silent, his eyes raw from crying.

Louis stood up as well. "I'll head up to the cafeteria and grab a drink, give you guys time to catch up."

"No!" Connor took hold of Louis's arm like a vice. "Don't go."

Louis glanced at Elliott, who met him with a curious expression. He sat down again, saying, "OK, Connor."

Elliott stayed for twenty minutes or so, chatting about neutral topics and catching Connor up on events at school. Talking for talking's sake. Connor sat on the bed with his knees tucked up to his chin, nodding vaguely as Elliott spoke. It was as if nothing were computing.

Louis walked with Elliott to the door.

"He's like a completely different kid," Elliott muttered sadly.

An alarm bell went off in Louis' mind. He steered Elliott out of Connor's earshot and said, "It's normal for him to be like this. Don't let that change your mind about Special Guardianship. He's going to need a stable home more than ever now."

Elliott smiled and clapped Louis on the shoulder. "Thanks, man. I think I needed to hear that. Take care of him, won't you."

Louis nodded and watched him leave the ward. He turned his attention back to Connor, who had returned to a foetal position on the bed. Louis went back into the room and took his seat again. An impulse made him lift his phone out of his pocket and create a new message. His thumb hovered over the name Rona in his address book. Then, as quickly as the first impulse had hit, he deleted the message and put his phone back. He returned to watching over Connor as he slept, hoping the boy found a modicum of rest.

* * * * *

Louis arrived home at seven in the evening. The hospital, in conjunction with he and Aliyah, had agreed to discharge Connor late that afternoon. There was nothing medically wrong with him at this point so it would make sense for him to return to the children's home. When they'd reached the car park, Connor asked to travel with Louis. Louis made it clear that his old grey Vauxhall

Astra would not compare favourably to the likes of Aliyah's and Elliott's more high-end vehicles. That elicited a faint smile from Connor.

The three of them had travelled back to Robin Hill. Jeanette was on shift and she welcomed Connor home with a big hug. Ariana and Jimmy made a brief appearance, Ariana giving Connor a kiss on the cheek and Jimmy touching fists with him. Having paid their respects, they drifted off back to the living room. Connor announced that he was going to get a shower then chill in his room for a bit. Before he had disappeared up the stairs, he had turned to Louis and Aliyah and thanked them.

Louis had taken himself from Robin Hill to the gym, where he had spent the next hour and a half beasting himself in an effort to purge the intense emotions of the last twenty-four hours. It had worked to a degree.

He knelt to pick up a carrier bag on his doorstep, wincing as his quads burned. A pair of Tupperware boxes containing rice and what looked like chilli con carne were inside, along with a Post-It note signed from Luke and Annie. Louis smiled gratefully and went inside. Luke had text him earlier to check in, having heard the latest via Annie. Sharlene had also messaged, reminding him she was there if he needed anything.

Louis set the bag on the worktop and put some food down for Gonzo, who hurried into the kitchen and began devouring it as soon as the bowl hit the floor. Louis portioned himself out some food and put it in the microwave to heat up. He was touched by the thoughtfulness of his team. It made him wonder whether there would be the same sense of team and family if he decided to move to Op Hollowpoint.

He sent Damien a text, letting him know he was back home.

Damien's reply came moments later: Company? Followed by a smiley emoji, a kissing face and a hugging emoji.

Louis sent a thumbs-up emoji back, ignoring the whispers in the back of his mind that prophesised doom. Damien just wanted one thing and, once he got it, he'd drop Louis just was fast as he'd dropped Amy. Luke would probably bet a Dairy Milk bar that it would be over before Easter. Or worse, maybe Damien would love-bomb him until he was hooked then exert the same malign control as Simon had done. He shook his head clear, took his food out of the microwave and started to eat.

* * * * *

Connor started awake, gasping for air. The bedroom was dark, save for slivers of streetlight that peeked through the gaps in the curtains. He fumbled on the bedside table for his inhaler and drew on it. His chest relaxed a little and he sat up in bed.

He'd been having a nightmare. Emma was walking away from him in a dark warehouse. He screamed desperately for her to wait for him, but she didn't turn. Her blond curls bounced about her shoulders as she got closer to a large metal door. Connor kept yelling for her, stretching out his arms and running as hard as he could, but he felt like he was wading through tar. At the last moment, she turned, revealing a cold, dead face.

Connor shuddered and swung his legs out of bed. He checked his phone, which told him it was one in the morning. Yawning, he padded across the room in his socked feet to the wardrobe for a hoody. He dug out a grey one, pulled it over his head and started back to bed.

On an impulse, he turned and went to the window. He peeked through the curtains and gazed into the dark night. In spite of the clouds, the moon still made its silvery presence known. A mist had descended, making the orange glow of the streetlights eerier. There was no noise at all, not so much as a passing car. Connor gazed into the gloom, wondering whether he might catch a glimpse of a fox. He thought of Louis and felt comforted, less alone. Between Louis and Aliyah, they had held him together these last few days.

Just then, he spotted something in the distance. Way past the drive, under one of the streetlights, he saw someone standing there on the pavement. Connor rubbed his eyes, straining to make sure of what he was seeing. He was too far away to make out details, but there was definitely a figure standing there staring at his window. Even with the black, nondescript clothing and a hood pulled well up to hide the face, the tall, powerful build made Connor sure the figure was a man.

Connor stepped back from the window, letting the curtains flop closed. He wondered whether to run down and tell the night staff. Maybe Ariana had given her details to some creep and he'd come to find her. Connor started towards the door but then rushed back to the window as he heard a car engine turn over. He peeked out of the window again, just in time to see the tail end of a red car speeding off in the direction of the main road. Frowning, Connor returned to bed and pulled the covers over himself.

CHAPTER 17

Louis awoke as he sensed a shadow fall over his face, followed by the clunk of a mug landing on his bedside table. He opened his eyes slowly, squinting at the light from the bedside lamp, and watched Damien moving round the bed in a pair of black boxer shorts, mug in hand.

"Hi," Louis murmured sleepily, sitting up. "What time did you get here?"

Damien slid back under the covers and sat shoulder-to-shoulder with him. "It was later on. Sorry I was so long, stuff to sort out. You were dead to the world."

Louis wasn't surprised. He'd left his door unlocked and told Damien to let himself in when he got there. He vaguely remembered feeling Damien's warm body joining him in bed at some point during the night, but had no idea when. All the same, it was a nice feeling to wake up to him.

"What time is it?" he asked closing his eyes and laying his head on Damien's shoulder. Today was their first early shift back after rest days. Not that it had been particularly restful, Louis thought grimly.

"Quarter-to-six," replied Damien. "I brought a set of blacks with me so I won't need to go home first. As long as you don't mind me borrowing your shower?"

Damien was referring to the black polo vests and cargo trousers response officers wore under their body armour and tac-vests. Louis sighed, searching for the motivation that would take him through the day. "It might actually be nice to deal with a straightforward theft-from-shop."

Damien chuckled. When he next spoke, his voice was hesitant. "Listen, about us…"

Louis' eyes snapped open. He was suddenly on high alert, his body tensed for whatever was about to follow.

Damien must have felt it because he slid his arm around Louis' shoulders and pulled him in closer. "Can we just keep this between us for now?"

From deep within the box of Simon-isms, a voice hissed, "He's ashamed of you."

Louis did his best to stay grounded in the moment but could only manage a terse reply. "Sure."

"Don't misunderstand me, Louis," Damien said, putting his mug down on the bedside table. "I'm not ashamed of being with you. But it'll be big news at work and I don't know if I'm ready for that yet. I need some time."

"I understand," said Louis, a little more reassured. Nevertheless, it didn't quite silence those whispers from the box.

Damien pulled Louis down the bed so he was flat on his back then leaned over him so they were chest to chest. He nibbled playfully at the side of Louis' neck, making him squirm to try and escape the ticklish sensation. Damien held him tighter, saying, "You sure?"

Louis slapped Damien across his meaty glutes in a bid to free himself. "Go get in the shower, idiot."

Damien took one last nip at Louis' neck then rolled off him and bounded out of the room. A moment later, Louis heard the shower running. He got out of bed and crossed the hall to the spare room for his clothes. Whilst he gathered a fresh set of blacks, he glanced out at Damien's distinctive red Mercedes in front of his driveway. It would only take Luke turning up unannounced for the secret to be out. He supposed that would be for Damien to deal with.

Louis sighed heavily. He decided to give Damien the benefit of the doubt. For an organisation that was intimately familiar with the Official Secrets Act, the force was constantly ablaze with gossip and rumour. Louis could appreciate why Damien might want some privacy whilst this relationship, if that's what it was, budded. Plus, there was something exciting about a little secrecy. Louis grinned at the thought of sitting in today's briefing with no one any the wiser to the fact that Damien had spent the night with him.

* * * * *

The shift began steadily enough. Louis was singled-crewed, normal for an early shift. He made the most of the quiet morning to collect various bits of CCTV footage and obtain witness statements for jobs on his workload. The team was back to full strength today, which made a big difference.

At around ten-thirty, he pulled into a coffee drive-thru for a drink and a chance to update some notes on his handheld terminal. As he typed, the device flashed up with a call from Aliyah.

"Hi, Louis," she said, sounding worried

"Everything ok?"

"Not exactly," she replied. "Connor's missing.....well, I'm not sure if that's the right word...."

"Tell me," Louis said, frowning.

Aliyah said, "I went up to Robin Hill today to see Connor. I wanted to talk to him about making some funeral arrangements for his mum. Anyway, the staff told me he wasn't there."

"He hasn't been reported missing," said Louis.

"I know. Elliott picked him up this morning, apparently to take him to school. I wouldn't have expected Connor to go in today, given what he's been through the last few days, but he went with Elliott all the same."

"So, he's done a runner from school?"

"That's just it! They never made it there." Aliyah's voice came across with an edge of panic. "I called them both, their phones are switched off. When I called the school, they told me Elliott is off sick today."

Louis' brow furrowed with concern.

"I started thinking about what was said at the strategy meeting the other day after that Bryan man was charged. You know, that there was someone else involved?" Aliyah continued. "What if something's happened to Elliott and Connor? Tell me I'm being stupid, Louis!"

Louis felt an icy pang of fear. "I don't think you are. Give me five minutes and I'll ring you back."

He ended the call and activated the messenger app on his handheld terminal. He searched for Karen Lucas and was relieved to see she was shown as being available. He sent her a message asking if he could call urgently. Within a moment, he was speaking to her on the phone and relaying what Aliyah had told him.

"Worrying," she murmured, gathering her thoughts. "Ok, Louis, we better make a start with tracking them down. Hopefully, there's nothing to be concerned about but let's not take chances. I'll contact the shift commander to organise some additional units to help. You head to Elliott Penton's house and see if there's any sign of them."

Karen was as good as her word. Within ten minutes, a missing person alert was being broadcast across the police radio and a unit despatching to Robin Hill to obtain an initial report. Karen had requested Automatic Number Plate Recognition enquiries for Elliott's car. The ANPR cameras dotted around the region read every numberplate that drove past them; if Connor and Elliott were travelling in Elliott's car, it would flag up within minutes.

Louis called Aliyah back quickly to update her, then obtained Elliott's address via his handheld terminal. Elliott's address was on the system from a theft he had reported a year ago. Louis cast his eye down the list of reports linked to Elliott; unsurprisingly, nothing of concern and all linked to work. He set off and travelled as quickly as he could without speeding. Times like this made him pine for a response-driving permit.

* * * * *

Twenty long minutes later, Louis pulled into a picturesque cul-de-sac called Mulberry Close. There were only five or six houses, smart red-bricked detached new-builds with pitched slate roofs. Elliott's was the fourth one in. Like all the others, it was well-presented on the outside. No sign of a car on the driveway though.

191

Louis parked up and got out. He went to the door and knocked loudly, before peering through the living room window. The room was furnished in a smart, minimalist fashion and nothing seemed out of place. Louis knocked on the door again before going round to the back of the house. The kitchen was tidy but with no signs of life. Louis turned his attention to the garage. He supposed it was possible that the car was parked in there.

"Is everything alright, Officer?"

Louis turned to find a middle-aged woman stood at the top of the driveway. An excited border-collie flitted around, looking for new and interesting scents. She pulled it gently towards her and shortened the leash as Louis approached. "I don't suppose you've seen the occupant today?"

"Elliott? No, not since this morning. He normally takes off fairly early anyway for the gym. Is everything ok?"

"Fine, thanks," Louis replied, smiling reassuringly. "Just following up on some enquiries regarding an incident at his workplace."

"That school," the woman groaned, shaking her head. "I don't know how he does it."

"Is there any chance his car might be in the garage?"

"No. Too full of gym equipment!"

Louis thanked her again and got back into his car. He updated the incident log with the result of his enquiry then sent the same update directly to Karen Lucas. She acknowledged his message but didn't task him with anything else.

Louis sat and thought for a moment. He didn't want to just sit here and do nothing, but nor did he want to cruise blindly through the city on a fool's errand. A flash of inspiration came a moment later.

After taking a second to make sure he wasn't talking rubbish, he sent a further message to Karen. Whilst waiting for her to acknowledge it, he checked the log again and noticed that there had been an update from the ANPR researchers with the last sighting of Elliott's car.

"What the fuck is going on?" Louis whispered to himself as he set the car in motion.

* * * * *

The sun shone brightly down on Garnett Street as Louis pulled in. Despite the sunshine and crisp blue sky, there was still a grimness to the place. Louis waved at two Police Community Support Officers as he drove past. Following recent events, the Neighbourhood Policing Team had upped its patrols of the area. He continued cruising around, dipping into the narrow side streets as well as the wider roads that led deeper into the industrial estate. The ANPR cameras could only give a rough indication on where Elliott's car might be, based on the location of the camera it triggered. When Louis saw the location, the only logical answer was that the car was somewhere near Garnett Street.

Louis passed a group of functioning warehouses and moved into a more derelict area, a combination of overgrown wasteland and crumbling skeletons of decaying buildings. In the distance, he saw the sprawling Low Dean Mills complex. Even in the sunshine, the place made Louis shudder.

His handheld terminal started ringing so he pulled over to answer it.

Karen Lucas' voice came over the line. "Louis, the telecoms results are back."

Louis waited for the news. Outside Elliott's house, he'd

remembered Connor talking about receiving messages from an unknown number purporting to be Emma. Based on the pathologist's initial report, it was highly unlikely that Emma was alive when those messages were being sent so the sender either had to be Hillesley or his accomplice. It might be that the accomplice had thought to switch off Elliott's and Connor's phones but left his on in the belief that the police didn't know about it.

"It's an unregistered pay-as-you-go SIM," said Karen. "It's pinging off a phone mast near your location, but we can't narrow it down much further. It's not an exact science, as you probably know."

"It has to be Low Dean Mills, Ma'am," Louis replied. "It's too much of a coincidence. Wait...!"

He tossed the terminal onto the passenger seat and drove the car left towards a cluster of overgrown bushes. As he rounded them, he braked and picked the terminal back up. "I've found the car, Ma'am."

* * * * *

Louis arrived outside the main gates to Low Dean Mills and got out of the car. He shouted up on the radio, advising the operator of his location. He had left Elliott's car with the two PCSOs he had passed earlier to guard, awaiting the arrival of a forensic recovery truck. Karen had agreed for him to head to the mills but strictly for recon only.

It was a tight squeeze, but Louis managed to fit through the gap in the gates. He scanned the yard and saw no signs of life. The sky was starting to cloud over, the breeze suddenly becoming chillier. He set off towards the front doors. His radio chirped and he answered it hurriedly. Luke's voice came over the point-to-point.

"Damo and I are on our way, mate. Sit tight until we get there."

Louis assured him that he would. A moment later, a point-to-point came from Damien. He and Luke were also single-crewed today so were travelling separately. "Everything ok?"

Damien's voice was clipped, focussed. Louis could tell that Damien was in cop-mode now. "All quiet. I can't see Connor anywhere."

"Keep your eyes open and don't go kicking any doors in until we get there," Damien warned him sternly. "Make sure your body-cam's on. ETA eight minutes."

The call dropped out as Louis reached the doors. Taking Damien's advice, he slid the switch down on his body-cam to activate it. He then tried the doors. Locked tight. He headed left, intending to walk the perimeter of the building. There had to be another way in.

* * * * *

Connor opened his eyes and tried to orient himself. He was laid on his side on a dank-smelling couch. As his vision adjusted to the gloom, it was clear he was in an old factory of some sort. The sound of dripping water echoed throughout the cavernous room. Shafts of sunlight beamed down like spotlights in certain places through holes in the ceiling. Connor felt drowsy, much like when he had woken up in Bryan's house.

His first instinct was to get to his feet. As he tried, he realised something was wrong and narrowly avoided smashing face-first into the floor. He looked down to his ankles and saw that they were bound together with duct tape. His wrists were restrained in a similar fashion behind his back. What to do next? If he shouted for help, it was unlikely someone would hear him. It might even bring whoever had done this to him. He took the chance all the same.

"Help!" His voice echoed through the room. He yelled again, louder this time. In the corner of his eye, he saw something stir in the shadows. It was moving painfully slow, like some sort of zombie.

"Elliott!"

Connor almost cried when he saw Elliott emerge from the shadows, dragging his leg behind him. He was hurt.

Elliott put his finger to his lips and knelt down in front of the couch, wincing in pain. "Quiet! She could be back any moment. We need to get out of here."

"What happened?" Connor whispered, trying to wriggle his wrists free of the duct tape. "We were talking in your car and then..."

"Later," Elliott whispered back. He produced a red-handled multi-tool from his pocket and flipped open the penknife. "This should do it."

Connor held still as Elliott rested one hand on his ankle and guided the penknife towards the duct tape.

He was just about to touch the blade to the bonds when he stopped suddenly. "Wait!"

Connor shot an anguished gaze at him as Elliott folded the penknife away. "Elliott?"

Elliott smiled brightly and brought himself closer to Connor's face. "Better idea. How about we keep you tied up whilst we have a little chat? Then, when we're finished, I choke the fucking life out of you?"

CHAPTER 18

Louis sauntered around the mill, not even a quarter of the way around yet. The building was vast but he didn't dare move too quickly in case he missed a way in. Overgrown bushes and corroded scrap metal lay everywhere, making it harder to spot a potential entryway. There wasn't so much as a window at a reachable level; any potential apertures were well and truly closed off with steel panels. It wasn't physically taxing but Louis was breathing hard, frightened for Connor's safety.

On second thoughts, he decided to risk speeding up. He could always double back if he completed a lap and found nothing. Damien had said eight minutes until he got there, and Luke wouldn't be far behind either. Knowing how the pair of them could shift a police car on a blue-light run, it wouldn't be much longer until there were two more pairs of eyes to search for a way in. In fact, they'd probably just take the front doors off with the red key. Meanwhile, he'd just have to keep looking.

* * * * *

"What the fuck is wrong with you, Elliott?" Connor wailed, thrashing about on the sofa. "Let me go!"

This was beyond insane. It was Elliott standing there, his teacher who had always been firm but fair. Always kind and encouraging but never letting him get away with any bullshit. Something must be wrong with him. Maybe someone had given him drugs to make him go crazy. Maybe he was having some kind of mental breakdown. Either way, he was standing there smirking as Connor wriggled on the filthy sofa that had, until very recently, seated his dead mother.

Elliott had picked Connor up that morning, telling staff he was taking him to school. Little did they know that Elliott had called Connor a short time before and offered to take him to where Emma had died in order to pay his respects. Aliyah would never let him see Emma's body, Elliott had told him, nor would she entertain him being involved in any funeral arrangements. Emma would be placed in a pauper's grave, unmarked and unloved. It was the final insult to injury.

Connor felt his chest tightening. He needed to calm down or risk an asthma attack. He wasn't sure if his inhaler was still in his pocket and, even if it was, he couldn't be sure that Elliott would give it to him. He stopped squirming and asked, "Why are you doing this? I thought you were OK!"

"Is that what you thought, you little cock-tease?" Elliott growled, starting to pace back and forth in front of the sofa. There was nothing wrong with his leg now, evidently just another cruel ruse. After a moment, he stopped and shouted, "I was going to give you everything! You would've come to live with me, you would have wanted for nothing and we would have been happy! But you fucked it up, Connor! As soon as you clapped eyes on that half-breed copper, I was no good for you anymore!"

Connor blinked, unable to comprehend the bile erupting from Elliott's mouth. "Elliott, I've got no fucking idea what you're on about!"

198

"Of course you don't!" he snapped. "It's a way of life for people like you and your slut mother. Never let go of one branch until you've got firm hold of another!"

The mention of Emma brought tears to Connor's eyes, tears of rage this time. Elliot's smile when he saw Connor weeping was one of pure pleasure.

He started pacing again. "I was a lot younger than you when my dad started bringing me to a place like this. He insisted it was just to pay off debts, but I soon found differently. He actually enjoyed passing me around his friends. Funnily enough, it would happen on a couch not dissimilar to this. I set fire to the fucking thing one day. I used so much petrol it took part of the building with it."

Connor started to look around, wondering what his options were. Elliott was getting increasingly wound-up. Connor didn't like the sudden foray into arson. If it was a choice between being raped or being set on fire, Connor knew which one he'd prefer. "If you want sex, Elliott, I'll do whatever you want. I won't tell anyone, I swear."

Elliott's laugh reverberated throughout the building. "I could have done that anytime. I could have done that at Bryan's place, come to think of it. We gave you a lot more ketamine than I have this time. That was your punishment, by the way, for straying from me. How could you make me do it though? I was determined to be better than my father. You were going to be mine alone. I wouldn't have let anyone touch you."

"I haven't done anything to you!" yelled Connor, tears rolling down his cheeks. "I don't know what you're fucking talking about!"

"No," Elliott replied gently. "You will, though."

Connor didn't know what else to do but scream for help once

more. Elliott laughed at him then came in close to his face and screamed in unison with him, his eyes bulging and the muscles in his neck flaring. He was truly frightening. Connor went silent, afraid to make any more noise in case it triggered Elliott to hurt him.

"It's over for you, Connor," he said, giving him a gentle kiss on his cheek. He drew back and smacked his lips together, savouring the taste of Connor's tears. "You're not leaving here alive."

Both of them jumped at the sound of glass breaking somewhere in the building, followed by a loud thud.

Connor opened his mouth to shout but Elliott was too quick for him. He forced Connor's face into the sofa cushion and held it there with his foot on the back of Connor's head whilst he retrieved the roll of duct tape. As he fastened a strip to Connor's mouth, he whispered, "Try not to have an asthma attack and die, will you? Because I am so looking forward to picking you up by your beautiful little neck and squeezing it until those baby-blue eyes pop right out of your fucking skull. And afterwards, I'm going to feed your rotting little carcass to those foxes that you and your boyfriend love so fucking much."

Connor gasped as Elliott grabbed him by the throat, lifted him partially off the couch for a moment then threw him back down. Suddenly, he was gone. Connor tried to regulate his breathing but it wasn't working. His chest was tightening and he knew he was on the verge of an asthma attack. Tears streamed down his cheeks. He knew he was about to die.

* * * * *

Louis picked himself off the filthy stone floor. He had spotted the unprotected window higher up the wall of the building. The remnants of an outdoor latrine shed had allowed him to scale up high enough to reach the window. He had used his baton to smash the glass out and peer inside. It was easily a twelve-foot drop with no means to shimmy down or break his fall. He couldn't quite see whether the floor was stone or wood. The last thing he wanted was to drop straight through the floor into the basement, more than likely breaking both his legs in the process.

He had been about to shine his torch downwards when he had heard Connor scream. Without another thought, he'd dropped through the window and hit the ground hard, rolling onto his side as he landed.

On his feet now, Louis gripped the handle of his baton tightly, laying the shaft across his upper arm as he drew it back ready to strike. He turned the volume of his radio right down in case a sudden transmission gave his position away. He advanced slowly through the passageway, the overpowering stench of damp filling his nostrils. There was barely any light but he didn't want to risk alerting whoever was in here by using his torch.

It occurred to him just then how stupid this plan was. He'd ignored advice from both Luke and Damien, and an order from Karen for that matter, about coming in here alone. Fuck it, he thought, taking another step forward, I'm here now.

The passageway led him into a cavernous room. He imagined that it would have been filled with loud, rattling machinery that processed the wool into textiles back in the day.

He scanned the room. A jerky movement to the left caught his eye. Connor lay on a dirty couch, thirty feet away. Louis checked his surroundings cautiously then darted forward. As he got closer, he could see that Connor had been bound and gagged.

In the same second that he saw Connor's eyes bulge emphatically, he sensed a swift motion behind him and twisted sharply. He felt the heavy impact of a metal pipe strike his shoulder. Had he not moved, it would have almost certainly caved his head in. His body armour dissipated a lot of the impact, but it was still enough to send him tumbling to the ground.

Before he could gather himself, Elliott was on top of him, teeth bared and bellowing obscenities. Louis couldn't even make out what Elliott was saying, such was the other man's rage as he screamed and sprayed Louis with spittle.

Elliott went for Louis' head first, determined to grab hold and smash it into the stone floor. Louis held his arms up defensively, preventing him from getting a grip. He bucked his hips hard to dislodge Elliott but he was too heavy. His training kicked in and he grasped for the orange button on the top of his radio, activating the Code Zero alarm.

Louis gasped as Elliott's hands suddenly found his throat. Before he could react, Elliott dug his thumbs deep into Louis' windpipe. Louis struck out with both his arms, making contact with the sides of Elliott's face. It wasn't enough. Elliott doubled down on the pressure, bringing his face closer to Louis' in the process. Finally, Louis understood what he was saying.

"I'm going to choke you to death, bastard," hissed Elliott. "And then, I'm going to throttle that little fucking rat over there on the sofa until he's as dead as you."

Louis tried to take hold of Elliott's hands and prise them off but he was too strong. A roaring noise started in Louis' ears. He wasn't sure if it was Elliott screaming at him or something else. Either way, his vision was blurring over. A sense of peace was washing over him. He couldn't quite feel his face anymore but he felt positive that he was smiling.

Then, the voices came. Damien's voice? Wait, no. Luke's voice. Shouting. Why the hell were they shouting? Elliott was still shouting, his face contorted with rage. Everyone was so fucking angry.

Elliott suddenly went bolt upright, his eyes bulging and his mouth forming into a shocked 'O'. Louis felt the pressure on his throat dissipate. He gasped, sucking in the air he so desperately needed. His vision cleared and the roaring in his ears subsided. Not quite stopped. Shouting. Damien.

"Don't move!" Damien yelled at the top of his voice.

Louis didn't know who he was talking to but he mustered enough strength to shove Elliott's body off him. It was only then that he saw two Taser barbs sticking out of Elliott's back. Louis' eyes followed the wires back to Damien, who stood ten feet away with his Taser outstretched. Damien didn't move a muscle until Luke had rushed forward and slammed his handcuffs onto Elliott's wrists in a rear-stack position.

Louis sat up and opened his mouth to say something, only to twist over to the right and wretch hard, throwing up his coffee from earlier that morning. He managed to raise himself to his hands and knees so he could crawl towards Connor. Damien intercepted him, his Taser now stowed back in its holster. "Slow down. You're ok."

Louis thrust his chin out in Connor's direction. Damien turned but Luke was already on his way to sit Connor up and remove the duct tape. As soon as his hands were free, Connor grabbed his inhaler and took several breaths.

Everyone turned towards the sound of a thunderous bang as the front door flew open and more uniforms charged in.

"You fucking idiot," Damien whispered, pressing his hand to Louis' face tenderly. "What did I tell you about kicking doors in by yourself?"

* * * * *

The next few hours were chaos. Louis felt like he was speaking to a blur of faces. Damien and Luke made way for Sergeant Khan, who made way for a pair of paramedics with torches that shone into his eyes. At some stage, Connor's face floated into view, only to disappear again.

He was blue-lighted to hospital in the back of an ambulance, only to have more lights shined in his eyes by doctors. Something was mentioned about petechial haemorrhaging but otherwise he was ok. A CSI technician flitted around him, taking photos of the bruising on his neck and shoulder, and of his eyes. A pair of detectives that he didn't know took him back to Weaver's Yard Police Station and deposited him in a family room. It was only at that point that he started to freak out. He needed to see a familiar face. Luke, Sharlene, Damien, anyone that could help him ground back into reality. He sat in one of the blue armchairs and cupped his face in his hands, not sure whether he wanted the tears to flow or not.

He looked up as he heard the door open. Sabina stood in the threshold, looking surprisingly tall in a black business suit and grey blouse. Connor pushed past her into the room and threw his arms around Louis' neck.

"You are a fucking legend, mate," he whispered.

Louis hugged him back tight.

Sabina dropped down into one of the free armchairs. "You two will be the sodding death of me."

Louis turned to her. "A lot of that going around lately."

He and Connor laughed at her vexed expression as she shook her head slowly. After a moment, she stood back up and put her hand on Connor's shoulder. "Time to go, love. We've got a date with the VRI suite. We'll need to keep you two separated until you've both given your statements."

Louis understood why but was grateful to know that Connor was ok.

Before he left the room with Sabina, Connor turned and said, "Lurch is waiting to talk to you too."

Louis smiled and stood up as Damien came in. As soon as the door closed, Damien threw his arms around Louis and buried his face into his neck. Louis held him tight, taken aback by the intensity of Damien's emotion.

"You are absolutely fucking crazy," Damien said finally, stretching out his arms to hold Louis in front of him. "I thought you were a fucking goner!"

"You and me both," said Louis.

"I can't stay with you," Damien said. "Luke and I are key witnesses to your attempted murder."

Louis blinked hard, the severity of the situation finally sinking in. "Shit."

"I know. Do you need anything before I go?"

Louis thought for a moment then kissed Damien softly on lips. "Just this."

CHAPTER 19

Louis paced around the family room, feeling more and more claustrophobic. He'd shed his body armour and tac-vest then tried to stretch out on the sofa to get some sleep. No chance. Every time he closed his eyes, the thumping noise in his ears grew louder. His neck was starting to feel stiff and swollen now. He was bored. The last human interaction he'd had was when two CID detectives came to take his statement.

He turned to the door as it swung open and smiled when he saw Luke enter, carrying a laptop under his arm. Luke set the laptop on the table, opened it up then turned and clipped Louis on the back of the head.

"Ow!"

Luke's face was stern. "I'll bloody ow you in a minute! Come here and watch this."

Louis came closer, wary of another slap. It was the body-cam playback app. "What is it?"

Luke didn't answer but clicked the play button. Louis knelt down and studied the screen. He saw Damien in the right hand of the screen and realised it was Luke's body-cam. They were running across the mill floor, the footage jiggling about wildly.

The couch came into view with Connor on it. A little further away, he recognised the black hoody Elliott had been wearing. He realised he was watching Elliott on top of him, choking him. Louis put a hand over his mouth as he watched his own body go from fighting back wildly to flopping on the ground. He could hear Damien and Luke yelling at Elliott to let him go. Damien was already drawing his Taser and shouting the required warning. Then a sudden pop and a crackle as the Taser discharged and delivered its incapacitating current to Elliott's body.

Luke shut the laptop and Louis stood up. "That was way too reckless, man. When we heard the Code Zero over the airwaves, we thought we were listening to you die. Me and Damo never moved so fast in our bloody lives!"

Louis didn't know what to say. When an officer activated the Code Zero button on their radio, it meant their life was in peril. All other transmissions were blocked for several seconds and every officer on shift would hear whatever sound was being picked up from their endangered colleague's radio. He'd heard it go off once before during shift handover. In a second, the report room cleared, everyone jumping into whatever van or car they could reach to rush to the officer's aid. The relief of being told to stand down because it was an accidental activation had been palpable.

"If anyone ever says Louis Mortimer doesn't have the balls to do this job, I'll see 'em," Luke said, smiling at last and drawing Louis into a one-armed hug. "Bring it in, brother."

Louis felt a lump in his throat. He took a moment before speaking. "What's going on? It's been hours."

The clock on the wall was approaching nine o'clock. For the first time that night, Louis thought of Gonzo.

"Karen Lucas is on the warpath, that's what," replied Luke, sucking air through gritted teeth. "She's going for a charge and remand on Elliott as we speak. Come on."

Louis followed him out of the family room and listened to Luke as they walked down the corridor.

"I've just been doing my statement," Luke said, "That's why I was re-watching the bodycam footage. Sabina Hussein's going to be interviewing him. Annie knows her. She's still pretty new in service, but she's bloody good."

They got into the lift and Luke pushed the button for the top floor. Once there, they headed down another corridor before passing through a glass door onto the roof. The chief superintendent had used some of the wellbeing budget to convert the flat roof into a pleasant outdoor space, even at minus two degrees.

Louis shivered as the cold air hit him, waking him up. Connor was already there, flanked by Aliyah and Sabina.

"He wanted to see you," muttered Luke as they approached the others. "Poor kid, I think he's feeling anxious."

"Can't say I blame him," Louis muttered back.

"The gang's all here," Aliyah said, smiling wryly. "Good to see you, Louis."

Louis returned her smile then said to Connor, "All done?"

He nodded and Sabina said, "Let's hope that's the last VRI you ever have to do."

"Luke says you're interviewing Elliott?" said Louis.

Sabina nodded. "I better go, actually. His solicitor said he'd be here for quarter-past nine. Are you going to stay for a bit?"

Louis nodded. Somehow, he didn't feel ready to go home just yet. He knew that as soon as he closed his front door, the enormity of today's events would finally hit him and he'd go to pieces.

Aliyah put her arm round Connor's shoulders. "We should be going though, mister."

"No chance!" Connor folded his arms across his chest and stuck his chin out obstinately.

"Connor, I'd like for you to spend at least one full night at Robin Hill," Aliyah replied sternly, crossing her arms as well. "Come to think of it, I wouldn't mind spending one full night in my bed without worrying about you. My family are starting to doubt that you're actually a teenage boy!"

"Well, if you take me back there I'm just going to....." Connor seemed to read the annoyed faces of the adults around him and decided not to finish that sentence. "Can't we just hang out with Louis for a bit?"

"Midnight," growled Aliyah, rolling her eyes. "That is the absolute latest! One minute more and I'm going to drag you by your curly mop back to Robin Hill."

"You're the best, Big Al," said Connor, baring his teeth in an exaggerated smile. To Louis, he said, "What is there to eat around here?"

Sabina rolled her eyes, laughed and set off back inside. They followed her as Luke took a point-to-point call from Sharlene. She was currently with Damien and two detectives searching Elliott's place.

They made their way back to the family room whilst Luke headed back to the report room to finish writing his statement. Aliyah and

Connor took a sofa each and Louis sat on the floor by Aliyah's sofa. Much to Connor's quiet amusement, both adults had closed their eyes in under ten minutes.

* * * * *

Sabina loved interviewing. The entire thing was somewhere between a wrestling match and a tango. Some partners were clumsy and unimaginative, some were sophisticated and exciting. Even someone who answered 'no comment' all the way through held an allure; the chance to press their buttons or make them slip up so they gave something away, Sabina lived for it. It made her feel excited and nauseous all at the same time. As she gazed across the table at Elliott Penton and his slick-looking solicitor Mr Arooj, she knew this would be a hell of dance. Her co-interviewer, DC Shirley Beck, stood up and activated the recording equipment.

"This interview is being audio and visually recorded and may be used in evidence if your case if brought to trial," Sabina announced in a clear voice. She gave the date, time and location of the interview before instructing everyone in the room to introduce themselves. Elliott was smiling at her in a way that made her skin crawl. "Elliott, you've been arrested for kidnap, child cruelty, making and possessing indecent images of a child and two counts of attempted murder."

Elliott scoffed and looked at his solicitor, rolling his eyes.

Sabina ignored the bravado. "I'm going to caution you now. You do not have to say anything, but it may harm your defence if you do not mention, when questioned, something which you later rely on in court. Anything you do say may be given in evidence."

She had no doubt he understood everything she had just said, but she took the time to explain anyway. She wasn't going to give him the opportunity to say in court that he hadn't known what she was saying. Just as she was about to explain the ground-rules for the interview, Arooj interrupted her.

"My client has a prepared statement for me to….."

"No, no, Mr Arooj," she said, smiling as she swiped her finger from left to right. She'd met enough solicitors who thought they could intimidate her because she was new, or because she was a woman. She had let them know in no uncertain terms that it was her interview, not theirs. Sabina finished her explanation of the ground-rules, looked over at Beck to ensure she was ready, then turned back to the solicitor. "Now you may speak."

She locked eyes with Elliott as Arooj started to read from the signed piece of paper on the table in front of him. Elliott's green eyes seemed to glow with eerie luminescence. His movie-star smile was dazzling. Sabina didn't doubt for a moment that if he could reach over the table and choke her to death, he would.

"My client denies any involvement or guilt in the offences put to him. He is a well-regarded school teacher, who has worked with the most vulnerable children for many years. These charges are nothing more than fabrications cooked up by a sexually-precocious child, who has been unduly influenced by a corrupt police officer seeking to exploit him for sexual purposes. My client has done nothing except help the boy and try to draw him away from these malign influences. From here out, he will give no comment to any further questions asked of him."

Sabina stared hard at Elliott as his smile widened. She let the silence hang for a moment, letting a little discomfort set in. Then she met his smile with one of her own, equally dazzling. She pulled her laptop onto the desk and opened it. A media player was already cued up.

"I'd like you to listen to this, Elliott," she said. "It's the Code Zero recording from the incident at Low Dean Mills, where you were arrested earlier today. Once you've listened to it, I'd like to know if there's anything you wish to say."

She hit play and immediately the room was filled with Elliott's screams of rage, a constant flow of obscenities as Louis gasped for air. Elliott's voice came across clear as he swore to strangle Louis to death, followed by Connor. The recording ended and Sabina's lips curled upwards as she saw Elliott's smile fade.

"Give me a moment," she said brightly, tapping on the laptop. "The next thing I'd like you to watch is PC Mortimer's body-cam footage, which shows you throttling a police officer as you scream your intention to murder him and then your fourteen-year-old pupil, who you have kidnapped, bound, gagged and forced to watch."

Elliott leaned over and whispered in Arooj's ear. Arooj then said, "My client requests a further private consultation with me."

Sabina smiled at Elliott and he met her gaze. "Yes, I thought he might. Interview suspended."

* * * * *

Connor started awake, blinking at the harsh fluorescent lighting in the family room. He'd been having the same dream of Emma again. He looked over from his sofa at Aliyah and Louis, who were both still dozing in the same places. He grinned at the sight of them. They were the most unprofessional professionals he'd ever met. No one would ever believe him if he described this scene.

A thought occurred to him and he stifled a chuckle. He tiptoed across the room. When he reached the other sofa, he lowered himself down next to Louis then pulled his phone out. He set it to selfie- mode, held it in his outstretched hand and snapped a couple of pictures of the three of them whilst pulling goofy faces. For the last one, he just smiled.

Connor settled back against the sofa and looked at the photos to see which one he liked best. They were all good. He smiled again, feeling a sense of comfort. He shuffled a little closer to Louis then folded his arms over his waist and closed his eyes again.

CHAPTER 20

They had all reassembled in the interview room and DC Beck set the recording equipment going again. Sabina ran through the formalities, reminding Elliott that he was still under caution.

"My client wishes to make an oral statement," announced Arooj. "However, he wishes you to know that he will be discussing intensely painful childhood memories that he has repressed for a great deal of time. He therefore asks that you do not interrupt him as he recounts them to you."

"Of course," said Sabina, marvelling at this little power-play. It was turning out to be quite a dance. "Please Elliott, in your own time."

Elliott took a deep, dramatic breath then began.

"My father....." Everyone waited as he appeared to muster himself. "My father abused me. And he did so in the most horrendous way."

He leaned forward and cupped his face in both hands. His body shook as loud sobs came forth. Sabina was unmoved. Beck pushed a roll of tissue paper across the table towards him. When Elliott recovered himself, he continued, "Imagine being so young, not knowing any better. Love and sex and pain all being twisted together. I never had a chance."

Elliott ignored Sabina and looked over at Beck, thanking her for the tissue. He dabbed his eyes. "When he made me go with other men to pay his debts, he said it was something I should do if I loved him. He said he hated asking me to do it. I used to believe him, you know? Every child wants to believe the best of their dad. Then I realised he was watching it happen and getting off on it. The worst thing was that I still loved him. He was my dad."

Sabina gritted her teeth as she watched him weep bitterly into the scrunched-up tissue. Unfortunately, she knew she would need to play his game for a bit. "I'm so sorry that happened to you, Elliott."

He sniffed hard and nodded. "You're more interested in things with Connor, though."

"I want you to get there in your own time," she replied gently.

"I fell in love with Connor when I first laid eyes on him. But not a bad love, you know? A fatherly love. He had a way about him that made me want to look after him. He's been with me for three years. That's a long time to know someone. I nurtured him. I brought him on."

Sabina nodded. "You're doing really well, Elliott. It's helping me understand."

"I know you're going to send me to prison," he sobbed, but this time with a cold edge behind it. "So, yes, I loved him like a father loves his son. The only problem is, when you've grown up with a father like mine...."

Sabina nodded emphatically.

"Everything gets twisted."

"Tell me about that, Elliott. How did it get twisted?"

"I wanted things from him that...." Elliott paused and scrunched the tissue hard in his hand, screwing his eyes shut. "That my father used to want from me."

"How did you deal with that?"

"I started talking to people like Bryan Hillesley on the Internet. Not the normal Internet, though. The dark corners of it, where it's easy to find people who think like me. And people who will sell you ketamine and have it delivered through your door like an Amazon parcel." He snorted with laughter at the thought of that. "I figured that I could just keep my fantasies in check by living them out with people on the Internet. I wanted to be a good dad to Connor."

"A good dad to him?"

Elliott looked up. "Oh, yes. I didn't say. I was in the process of applying for a Special Guardianship Order. You know, make him mine legally. No more social workers, no more foster carers. Just the two of us together."

"Like a couple?"

"A family," Elliott corrected her. "But yes, there was part of me that wanted that too. In time, Connor would have realised he felt the same way about me too."

"So, what happened, Elliott? How did we get here?"

"Connor's immature," replied Elliott, tearing little squares off the tissue as he spoke. "You probably know about his mum, right? I'm sure she did her best, but come on, how was Connor ever going to know how to have a functional relationship when he's got a junkie whore for a mother?"

Sabina resisted the urge to grit her teeth. "Go on."

"It was too easy for his head to be turned. Look how quickly he glommed onto *him*." There was venom in Elliott's voice as he referred to Louis. "Who knows, maybe he was curious about those unfortunate racial stereotypes and wanted to see for himself..."

Elliott looked up at Sabina and she knew he was searching for a reaction. She gave him nothing. "So, you felt that he was being unfaithful to you?"

"Yes!" cried Elliott. "Maybe not with his body. Not yet, anyway. But certainly in his mind. I've seen it before. What made it worse, *Louis* was desperately trying to be my friend. Well, more than that actually. They can't get enough, that lot."

Sabina felt herself gripping her pen tightly. She was pretty certain that Elliott wasn't genuinely racist; more likely, he was trying to upset or anger her for his own pleasure. "You mentioned people like Bryan Hillesley. Tell me about that."

"There were a few," said Elliott. "Bryan had a thing for boys like Connor. Over time, I turned him onto the things that I needed to manage my own urges."

"Violence?"

"Yes. We'd roleplay online. I was his blue-eyed boy. Sometimes I'd behave well. Sometimes I'd behave badly. That's when things got interesting."

"So, you essentially roleplayed yourself as Connor?"

Elliott nodded. "I thought it would help me understand him better. Well, that was part of it. I'm sure in this kind of job, you've heard of children who have involuntary physiological reactions to sexual abuse? After enduring years of men beating me and choking me, my own father included, it became an integral part of my own sexual behaviour."

Elliott looked down at the table for a moment, pensive, then met Sabina's gaze again. "There's something quite….intimate...about choking someone, you know? That special moment when you look into each other's eyes, right before the spark goes out in theirs. Yours is the last touch they feel before it all goes dark."

Sabina saw Elliott shudder. She strongly suspected it was more through excitement than revulsion. The reasoning behind his decision to strangle Louis and Connor was now all too clear. "Tell me about any links between Bryan and Connor."

"You could say I set them up," Elliott grinned. "I pretended to be Emma, sending Connor the odd text to hook him. He told me once that she used to call him CJ. No one else calls him that. It was easy to persuade him. Just like it was easy to encourage him to go missing from his foster placements and look for her. That was me, by the way. I figured that the more dysfunctional I made him, the more eager Social Services would be to support my application for Special Guardianship."

Sabina deliberately echoed his words, trying to get him to expand. "So, you set Connor and Bryan up?"

"Yes," said Elliott. "I could have told Connor to go anywhere, but there was something so ironic about making him get into a car in the red-light district. Like mother, like son. Bryan had never done anything like this before but I persuaded him it would be fun. We used the roleplays like rehearsals. I told him how much ketamine to use, how often. I waited until Connor was out cold before I came into Bryan's house. I didn't want him to see me."

"And you left before he woke up?"

"Actually, I went back home to collect a few things. I'd planned to make a night of it with Bryan and Connor. When I came back to Bryan's though, the place was swarming with police so I drove off."

"What did you plan to do?"

Before Elliott could answer, Arooj put a restraining hand on his elbow. A tacit signal not to answer. Elliott glanced at him then turned back to Sabina and smiled. "Nothing. I just watched Bryan have some fun and made sure he didn't go too far."

"What I don't understand," said Sabina, sitting back in her chair and tapping the end of her pen against her lip, "Is why you allowed this to happen to Connor? After all, you've just told us that you were keen not to repeat your father's patterns."

Elliott nodded approvingly. "You've been listening. It was partly a punishment but also part of the wider strategy. Once Bryan had had his nasty way with him, Connor would go off the rails even more. Maybe he'd even be a little more receptive."

"Punishment?"

"And you were doing so well. When I realised he was starting to flirt with his new friend, I wasn't about to let that go. The final nail in the coffin was at the hospital. Connor made it clear whose bed he wanted to lie in. That's when I decided on our little road trip to Low Dean Mills. Don't get me wrong, it wasn't an easy choice to make. Do you know, I stood outside that children's home for ages that night, wondering whether I was doing the right thing?"

"I guess it was a big decision," Sabina said. "So, your motivation for the offences against PC Mortimer was that you felt Connor was being unfaithful to you with him, at least in spirit?"

Elliott sat back in his seat, smiled and replied, "I've said all I'm going to say. There was no intention on my part to do PC Mortimer or Connor any serious harm or to kill them. Anything that might have been said was in the heat of the moment. There was no intent behind it."

"I see," said Sabina, putting her pen down. "Well, thank you Elliott, I think we'll end the interview there for now. We may wish to speak to you again in a little while. I assume Mr Arooj will want to have a brief consultation with you?"

Arooj nodded and she and Beck left them in the interview room after turning off the recording equipment. When they were out of earshot, both women let out a long sigh of relief.

"Jesus," whispered Beck. "He's absolutely nuts!"

"I know," replied Sabina, shaking her head. She felt like she needed to get into a bath and scrub her skin until the soiled feeling washed away. "He's a textbook sexual sadist. Do you know what the worst part is?"

Beck shook her head.

Sabina looked at her sternly. "I did some research with a little help from Connor's social worker. There were concerns about Elliott's behaviour throughout his childhood. Nothing to bring him to the attention of the police, but still worrying nonetheless. Here's the kicker, though. Elliott's dad died when he was three. All those perversions he's described, he got there on his own."

"You mean he's just fed us a load of flannel?" Beck gasped. She regained her composure and regarded her colleague. "He's a proper psychopath, isn't he? I suppose you'll want to put all this to him?"

Sabina smiled. "Oh yes."

* * * * *

Louis felt a hand on his shoulder, shaking him awake gently. He opened his eyes and jumped when he saw Karen Lucas leaning over him. He was still in the family room. Aliyah was asleep on the couch and Connor was sat beside him on the floor, snoring softly. Karen pressed her finger to her lips and beckoned him to follow her.

When they were outside the room, she said, "I heard you were having a little slumber party down here. Come with me."

She led him down to the custody block in the bowels of the building. It was eerily quiet tonight, no banging or anguished cries. They reached the charging desk, a raised stone block with a Perspex shield that protected the dour-looking custody sergeant behind it. An electronic screen was sunk into the forward-facing aspect of the desk so that prisoners could read what they were being charged with. Rather than walking up to it, Karen put a hand on Louis' shoulder and steered him to the far corner of the room, well away from the charging desk.

"Whatever happens," she said, "Stay here and don't say a word."

Louis heard a door swing open followed by footsteps, heavy boots and the click-clack of heels. From the corridor on the right, Sabina and a detention officer emerged with Elliott between them. He looked terrible. He was wearing a grey custody-issue tracksuit and foam slippers. His eyes looked blackened from lack of sleep and his hair was flat and greasy. They walked him to the charging desk and stood him in front of the monitor.

Sabina turned to him and said, "Elliott, you're going to be charged with the following offences. Kidnap, two counts of attempted murder, child cruelty, arranging or facilitating commission of a child sex offence, administering a noxious substance, possession and creation of indecent images of children."

She followed with the caution. "You do not have to say anything, but it may harm your defence if you do not mention now anything which you later rely on in court. Anything you do say may be given in evidence."

She read the particulars out for each offence, a legal requirement for charging someone. Louis watched in admiration as she read them out in a stern, even tone.

The custody sergeant spoke next. "Mr Penton, you've heard the charges against you. Do you wish to make any reply?"

Elliott turned and smiled at Louis. It was a twisted smile that dripped with hatred. He returned his attention to the custody sergeant. "I love you, Connor."

Louis shook his head in disbelief. That would form part of the official records. Connor would hear it in court. Mind games to the end, he thought. He watched as the detention officer led Elliott back to his cell to await transport to court in the morning.

* * * * *

A convoy of cars left Weaver's Yard Police Station a little after quarter-to one in the morning. Louis' grey Astra was sandwiched between Damien's red Mercedes to the rear and Luke's black 4x4 Kia. Sharlene's blue Ford Fiesta led the way and was the first to peel off towards the southbound ring-road. Aliyah's Mini Cooper was next, heading in the direction of Robin Hill to drop Connor home. The three of them cruised along the main trunk road towards the semi-rural suburbs.

The city was quiet, still. Louis' eyes were drawn to the bright full moon in the sky, which made the plumes of smoke rising from the chimneys of the distant factories look all the more dramatic. Louis skipped idly through his music playlist via the controls on his steering wheel, waiting to hit on something suitable. He settled for Sam Sparro's 'Black & Gold'.

The industrial buildings and tower-block flats soon slipped into the background, the straight road becoming slower and more winding. Older stone houses lined the road. Very few lights were on inside. Normal people keeping normal hours. Louis glanced in the rearview mirror at Damien's car and smiled. These had been a crazy few days.

As they neared the turn-off for Louis' estate, he began to wonder whether Damien would drive on with Luke or follow him home. Louis truly hoped for the latter. After today's events, he really didn't want to be on his own, inevitably ruminating on how close he'd come to death. There would be time enough to process that trauma. Just for tonight, he wanted to lay wrapped up in Damien's arms and feel safe.

Sighing, he flicked on his indicator and got ready to turn. He flashed his headlights twice at Luke, who responded by flashing his hazards a few times before disappearing round the bend. Louis smiled brightly as he saw Damien's car turn into the road and follow him home.

They parked up and went inside. Gonzo was prowling near his bowl in the kitchen. Louis quickly dished him out some food before grabbing two glass tumblers and a bottle of Jack Daniels from a cupboard. He held it up for Damien to see as he walked in from hanging his jacket up in the hallway and kicking off his boots. Louis half-expected a lecture for offering a Scotsman bourbon but none came. Damien accepted the large measure that Louis poured him. They clinked glasses and each took a healthy sip.

Louis coughed. His throat still felt swollen and sore. He looked over at Damien, who was studying him with an amused grin. Louis walked over and wrapped his free arm around Damien's neck, drawing their foreheads together. He playfully nuzzled Damien's nose with his as he asked, "You staying, then?"

Damien kissed him hungrily, a resounding yes.

CHAPTER 21

Louis groaned softly as he woke up. His head throbbed almost as much as his neck and shoulder. He was laid on his belly, face half-buried in the pillow. He opened one eye and spotted the significantly-depleted bottle of Jack Daniels on his bedside table. They had certainly hit it hard. Louis twisted his head the other way to gaze at Damien's sleeping form. He was laid on his back, snoring gently. Shafts of sunlight were peeking through the curtains but didn't seem to be disturbing him. As Louis reached out to drape his arm over Damien's waist, a pair of green eyes snapped open and glared at him. Gonzo had made himself quite comfortable on top of Damien's body, draped across his torso with his front paws resting on Damien's left collarbone.

"So, you approve?" Louis whispered, rubbing Gonzo's head. Gonzo eventually stood up, stretched and jumped off the bed. Louis watched the top of his tail swish round the bed and out of the door. He snuggled closer into Damien, laying his head down on his chest. The steady thump of his heart soothed him. Damien murmured sleepily and wrapped his arms around Louis.

Louis took full advantage of the extra warmth. He wasn't used to sleeping naked in this cold weather, even with such a thick duvet. Things had gotten physical very quickly last night. On Louis' part, it had been something extremely life-affirming: the heat, the intensity, the pleasure all conspired to help him forget that only a few hours ago, Elliott had almost killed him. For Damien's part, Louis could sense the urgent need to be close to him. He had been insatiable, as if letting go of Louis for just a moment might see him lost.

Louis allowed his hand to cruise idly down Damien's chest, over the ridges of his abs, and grazed the taut skin around his belly button with his fingertips. He pondered his first impressions of Damien; cold, brooding, detached. It led him to think of Simon, who had used sex as part-reward, part-weapon. For Simon, it was something else to grant or withhold depending on whether he felt Louis was toeing the line or not. Damien had been open, generous and warm.

An impulse struck Louis and he rolled away from Damien to pick his phone up from the bedside. Lying on his belly, he started a new text message. He hesitated for just a moment before pressing send. He sighed heavily, feeling a weight lifting.

"Come back here, you." Damien's eyes hadn't opened but he reached out and pulled Louis back into him, rolling on his side to spoon him. "Stay here a bit longer. I'll go get us a McGravil's breakfast in a bit."

Louis put up no resistance. McGravil's was the best independent bakery in town. He closed his eyes, allowing himself to drift off to sleep again.

* * * * *

It was nearly lunchtime when Louis parked up at Robin Hill. Aliyah and Connor were already in the car park. Connor had his black hoody pulled up to protect his ears from the biting wind, his blond curls poking out from all angles. It was just a flying visit. Aliyah had messaged earlier to say Connor was asking after Louis in that nonchalant way that meant he was actually quite anxious. Louis offered to pass through on his way.

"Alright?" Connor smiled wryly, touching his fist to Louis'.

"Yeah. Are you? Did you get some sleep?"

"He's only been up half an hour," scoffed Aliyah.

Connor tutted. "I've been traumatised."

She cuffed him gently on the back of the head then said to Louis, "How are you? It was a late night."

Louis stifled a grin. "Yeah, I guess it was. I'm ok."

"Any news from court about him?"

Connor scowled. "You can say his name. He's not the bogeyman."

"Elliott's pleaded not guilty," replied Louis. "They've remanded him to prison until his trial. It's set for six months from now."

Aliyah shook her head sadly. "Idiot. He's going to put you all through a trial. And for what?"

"It'll be fine," Louis said reassuringly. He changed the subject. "What are you guys doing today?"

"Funeral directors," Connor murmured, looking down to the floor.

Aliyah put her arm round his shoulders. "We're going to make sure Emma has a proper send-off."

Connor shrugged. "It'll only be us two there."

"Seven," Louis corrected him. "I'll be there. Sabina's coming. Sharlene and Luke too. And you better be putting on plenty of food. You've seen the size of Lurch? He likes his scran."

"I suppose we could stretch to a couple of pasties," Connor grinned. He looked down again and dragged the toe of his trainer back and forth across the gravel. "Thanks, man. You're alright."

They started walking over to Aliyah's car. She gave Louis a kiss on the cheek then got into the driver's seat. As the engine fired up, Connor turned to Louis and regarded him suspiciously. "You two aren't starting a thing, are you?"

Louis laughed and shook his head, amused as always by his directness.

"Good," said Connor. "Too fucking weird if you did."

Louis reached over and pulled the car door open for him.

Connor slid in and pulled on his seatbelt. Just as Aliyah was setting off, he wound the window down and smiled mischievously. "Lurch seems pretty into you though."

Too smart for his own good, Louis thought, grinning and shaking his head as he watched the Mini drive off.

* * * * *

Louis made the thirty-minute drive across the city to the Guildford Hill housing estate. Backing onto greenbelt land, the eighties-style estate was built around two beige-coloured tower blocks that dominated the skyline. Louis drove slowly through the narrow streets until he reached an unassuming semi-detached house. The waist-high wooden fence had seen better days but the garden was well-kept. Louis felt a little flutter in his stomach. There were no lights on. His rational brain kicked in. Why would there be? It was the middle of the afternoon! Rona had said she'd be in.

After switching off the engine, he pulled out his mobile phone to check messages and to reassure himself that Rona hadn't suddenly cancelled. Damien had sent him a photo message via Whatsapp. He was lying back in his bed, bare chest exposed, with a seductive smile and mischief in his blue eyes. "Post-shift plans?"

Insatiable. Louis sent him back a winking emoji followed by a kissing one, grinning as he did it.

He pondered for a moment, tapping the edge of the phone against his knee. Then he opened up his recent calls list and selected the number he wanted.

"Louis," Karen Lucas answered warmly. "Everything ok?"

"Yes, thanks, Ma'am," he replied. "I um...think I'd like to take you up on the offer of coming over to Op Hollowpoint."

"Excellent!" she cried. "Leave it with me, I'll make the arrangements. You've made the right choice. See you soon."

The call ended and he slid his phone back into his pocket. He got out of the car and walked to the garden gate. It groaned as he unlocked the catch and pushed it open. As he walked down the stepping-stone path, it occurred to him that Connor would be at the funeral director's now, making arrangements to bury his mother. Louis swallowed hard, the thought suddenly bringing with it a swell of emotion. He came to the side door and dabbed his eyes dry on the cuff of his jumper, hoping that the bruising on his face and neck didn't look too prominent.

A moment after he knocked, the door swung open and a fug of warm air and spicy food hit him. A diminutive woman with long, dark-brown hair tied up in a messy bun stood before him, her tight blue jeans and black baggy jumper emphasising her skinny frame.

The thought of Connor in the funeral parlour returned. Louis felt his lip quiver, his eyes welling up again. He just about managed,

"Hi, mum."

Sharona Mortimer, or Rona to her friends, reached her arms out and took hold of him gently by the shoulders. Her dark eyes lingered on his bruises.

"Come on, love," she said gently, drawing him into a hug as his shoulders started to shake. "I can see you've been in the wars."

He allowed her to guide him inside and close the door, happy to be home.

END

ACKNOWLEDGEMENTS

It would be wrong for me to end this book without acknowledging some of the most remarkable people and events that have allowed me to write it.

My career in safeguarding started quite by accident when I applied for a job working with boys and young men at risk of child sexual exploitation. I'd never worked with children before, so I was convinced I wouldn't be successful. In fact, I'd already lined up a job as a funeral director at my friend's chapel of rest. To my great surprise, I passed the interview with flying colours. So began my journey into child protection and safeguarding vulnerable people.

I mention this not to blow my own trumpet but to add weight to what I say next. It has truly been my honour to offer help to some of the most vulnerable people in our society. Although Connor is a fictional character, he is born from the energy and resilience of so many children who have not only survived terrible circumstances, but have also thrived in spite of them.

I am also privileged to work with so many brave and dedicated professionals, who tirelessly offer care and protection to those who need it most. I know from firsthand experience that there are so many police officers, social workers, doctors, nurses and teachers who don't go home until the job is done; characters like Louis, Luke and Aliyah are written with you in mind.

My thanks go to Tony Watts and Jacqueline Golding for mentoring me on this writing journey. Your guidance and support have helped turn a dream into a reality.

I'm grateful to various friends and colleagues (Allan in particular), who have encouraged me and fielded my technical questions at all hours of the day and night.

A special mention to Sam, literally my number-one reader, who spurred me on to the finish line.

Thank you, Donna, for always being proud of me.

To my parents, Dinesh and Fawzia, thank you for always supporting me whether near or far.

My brother Shakeel, gone but never forgotten.

To Anna, this book came about as we started our journey. Wherever it ends, thank you.

Gypsy, you are an antisocial, floofy menace but thanks for staying up late with me.

My final thanks go to Chris, my wonderful, long-suffering husband and accomplice in all things. I plead insanity!

About the Author

The world that Roshan Pitteea writes about is one he knows well.

A born-and-bred Northern boy, he is the son of two nurses who moved from Mauritius in the late '70s for work. Roshan grew up in Bradford, West Yorkshire: his love of reading, and of story-telling, began at an early age, and he went on to complete an undergraduate degree in European Politics at the University of Leeds.

Early on in his career he began working with victims of crime, which led him to apply for a job with a project aimed at safeguarding teenage boys from child sexual exploitation. This, he says, was the turning point in his career. The role took him into schools... but also into police-stations, prisons, brothels and red-light areas.

Working as a carer in children's homes to make ends meet, he went back to studying and was awarded a Masters with Distinction in Social Work.

Roshan began his career as a child protection social worker for a large Local Authority, working with vulnerable children and families experiencing abuse and deprivation. He quickly attained Advanced Practitioner status due to his work on a number of complex cases. He also developed a specialism for interviewing and assessing child sex offenders, consolidating this with a Post-Graduate Certificate in Forensic Psychology & Behavioural

Analysis.

After eight years in social work, Roshan decided to seek out a new challenge, and attested as a Constable for one of the largest territorial police forces in the North with the intention of becoming an accredited detective. He spent a year in uniform as a response officer before landing his dream role as a trainee detective on a Safeguarding Team.

Roshan completed his detective and specialist child abuse investigation accreditations in quick succession. He investigated serious and complex crimes against children and adults, often securing significant sentences against those responsible. He currently runs a specialist unit within the force, having achieved the rank of Detective Sergeant.

With his love of creative writing and a fertile imagination that skews towards the macabre, a book like *Care & Control* from Roshan was inevitable. He has used his knowledge of social work, psychology and crime to develop authentic characters who move within a gritty backdrop that will feel familiar to anyone who knows the North of England.

Roshan is clear that his work is neither autobiographical nor based on true stories, but hopes that his readers will feel the same energies of the people and places that have inspired him so profoundly.

He has started writing at a time where policing, social work and UK public sector services in general are facing significant challenges; and he hopes that, through his work, he can pay tribute to the dedicated people who work so hard to protect some of the most vulnerable members of society.

Care & Control , he says, is just the beginning...